Also by Ev Bishop

Bigger Things

Wedding Bands (River's Sigh B & B, Book 1)

Hooked (River's Sigh B & B, Book 2)

New Year's Resolution: One To Keep
(A River's Sigh B & B novella)

Writing as Toni Sheridan

The Present

Drummer Boy

EV BISHOP

Spoons

River's Sigh B & B, Book 3

SPOONS
Book 3 in the River's Sigh B & B series
Copyright © 2016 Ev Bishop

Print Edition

Published by Winding Path Books

ISBN 978-1-77265-000-6

Cover image: Kimberly Killion / The Killion Group Inc.

To Jen and Ang—

If I dedicated every book I wrote to you guys
it would be well deserved, yet still wouldn't
adequately show how grateful I am for your
expert help, kind encouragement, and
constant support.

Thank you so much for everything, but
especially for being such dear friends
throughout my writing journey and in life.

Chapter 1

NOELLE'S GIRDLE CHEWED AT THE flesh under her ribcage and the chub at the top of her thighs. And speaking of thighs, an itchy friction rash was forming. How on earth could her legs chafe when she wasn't even walking? *Good times.* Sweat trickled under the unintentional cleavage bursting forth from the cotton V-neck she'd thought would travel well—thought wrong. Over the barren miles of highway, it became a stretched out, shapeless mess, like the rest of her come to think of it.

Eva and Emily, thank God, had finally stopped their incessant bickering and the manic buzz of some cartoon was the only sound blaring from the middle seat in the minivan. Normally she, and they, insisted they sit on separate bench seats, but the van was packed so full this trip, they had to share. The horror, the outrage!

When she was a kid, she and Melissa—Oh, God, sometimes the small, silly memories hurt the most, like her heart was being peeled—and their two brothers had traveled smashed into a big station wagon, sweaty legs sticking to the vinyl seats, miscellaneous elbows jabbing tender bits, not a gaming device or portable DVD player in sight. And yes, she used to walk to school up hill both ways, too. Her inner attempt at humor didn't make her smile.

Noelle remembered those cramped road trips as happy times—or she did now, by comparison. Full of takeout chicken, raucous sing-alongs, and the glory of arriving at their destination, welcomed by their cousins and grandparents like they were long-lost, beloved relations, instead of people who lived just hours away and visited every holiday and random weekends too. So the beloved bit was true then, wasn't it?

The white noise of the tires and the hazy blur of passing scenery didn't have its usual soporific effect. Everything about this trip was the opposite of her family's holidays those long years past. It was just her, the girls, and Cade. Except when punctuated by fighting—the kids' or her and Cade's—it was quiet. Dull, if she was generous. Joyless, if she was blunt.

And this second leg of their twenty-hour drive wouldn't end with family fun to look forward to. Family would be there, yes, but at best, Cade and his parents and brothers tolerated each other. At worst, well . . . they were strangers, weren't they? Cade had left after the last big blow out and said he was never going back. So why *were* they going to Greenridge? She'd asked, of course, but he'd just shrugged and muttered that a thirty-fifth wedding anniversary was nothing to sneeze at.

Noelle wasn't so sure. Once she would've whole-heartedly agreed, but now she didn't know if thirty-five years of marriage should be honored if it was the loveless, soulless union her in-laws were mired in.

She sighed heavily. Man, it was hot. So hot. They should've stayed one more night at the hotel and got the air conditioning fixed. She glanced at Cade. His knuckles were white on the steering wheel, and his well-muscled arms were taut. He always reminded her of a Viking or something, bear-like in size, with tawny hair, skin that turned honey brown with even the slightest sun, and glacier blue eyes. She hated that after all they'd been through, she still thought he was the most attractive man she'd ever met. Did he even look at her anymore? Did he see her at all?

She sighed again, but Cade didn't so much as blink to register she'd made a sound. Nothing new there, either. When had he stopped asking if she was okay? Ah, well, it didn't matter. It wasn't like she was beating down any doors to find out what latest thing was stressing him out. And in some ways she didn't blame him for kyboshing the extra hotel night to fix the air conditioning. It wasn't the expense, not at all. Of all the marital stresses they could lay claim to, money issues weren't one of them. It was sharing confined space that was tough. The hotel only had one room left, and even though they'd slept in separate beds, Emily tucked in with her, Eva on the couch, the room was awkwardly intimate.

She shoved the last thought away and wondered, not for the first time, if their financial ease wasn't almost a curse itself. She had appreciated and fueled Cade's determination to get ahead, but what if that hadn't been their primary focus? Scraping by financially took a toll on a relationship, yes, but maybe the reverse was true, too. Maybe too much affluence had its own price. Maybe if they hadn't been so focused on money and accumulating things, they would've risen to the challenge of being each others' source of pleasure, comfort, entertainment, etc. and avoided this complete disconnect. No, she was just making excuses. For them both. As usual.

She fidgeted. Cade still ignored her, his eyes intent on the road. How was it, she wondered, with him always focused on where they were going, that they'd gotten so far off track?

She turned her head, willing away tears. Trees, trees, and more trees whipped past. How was she going to make it through the next month? And why did Cade insist on them staying for so long? If his reasoning behind the trip was unsatisfactory, his explanation for the trip's duration was bizarre—especially timing wise. Who announces a big family vacation right after his wife asks for a separation?

"I just don't get it," she'd said for the umpteenth time before they left. "Pretending for a moment I understand your burning desire to have your first visit home in years coincide with some big dramatic anniversary shindig, why on earth does it have to be for so long? It's way too much, and the kids will miss the first weeks of school."

His response had been weary and resigned, like he considered talking to her some almost-too-heavy cross to bear. "I just want one more vacation with the girls while they're young. Is that so much to ask? I want them to visit their grandparents, to get to know them a bit, before everything changes."

Noelle's eyelids were heavy and she was finally, mercifully, about to nod off when a bouncing motion in the backseat jolted her back to consciousness.

Emily was twisting in her seatbelt, peering at something out the window, and vibrating with excitement in that way only small children can, going from dead asleep to high alert in a heartbeat. "That was the sign. That was the sign!"

Her high-pitched glee sent a fire bolt of pain into Noelle's brain.

"We're almost there, Mom. Right, Dad?" Emily yelled at top volume.

"Inside voice, please," Noelle said, about to add that yes, it was exciting, but Cade interrupted.

"She's just happy. She's not hollering to bug you."

"Yeah, Mom. I'm just happy," Emily parroted, and Noelle wanted to leap out of the vehicle. Cade was still talking to the girls.

"Just wait 'til you see this place, guys. You'll love

it." Cade's voice couldn't have been warmer—and it hammered yet another nail into the coffin of their marriage. Noelle knew it made her a fundamentally bad person, or at least the kind of person she didn't want to be, but she was jealous of her daughters. No matter how things deteriorated between her and Cade or how distant he was from her, he was always there for his kids with every fiber of his being. It was one of his good qualities too, of course, but sometime in the past year or two she'd been left out and hadn't been able to get back into the circle.

She wouldn't change his love and support for the girls one iota—that wasn't really necessary to say, was it? She hoped it wasn't. Maybe it was something she needed to repeat like a mantra. You do not begrudge your children their father's love. You do not begrudge your children . . . and she didn't. She really didn't. But she also didn't like how he so easily and so consistently undercut her authority. Sometimes they'd even look at him after she'd issued a direction, as if to confirm that yes, they had to listen to her. And all too often he did what he'd just done now: joke it away or dismiss it, like he was somehow defending them from her when whatever she was asking for was perfectly reasonable.

If you'd told her in their early years together that one day she'd curse—or envy, at least—the very thing she loved most about him, she would've called you an idiot or worse.

She struggled upright, grabbed a container of citrus-scented wet wipes from the floor, and waved them over the backseat.

"Wake your sister," she said as Emily took the wipes. "And clean your face and hands and straighten your hair. We don't want Nan and Pops to think we're a bunch of ragamuffins."

Was it her imagination or did Cade grip the steering wheel even tighter? What did he want from her? She was so sick and tired of always having to guess what was crawling through his head.

In the backseat, Eva scrubbed her eyes blurrily.

"Don't!" she shrieked as Emily jabbed her in the ribs.

"Mom told me to wake you up."

"I'm already awake, stupid."

"Don't call me stupid. *You're* stupid."

And with that oh-so-witty comeback, the fight was on. Doing her best to tune out the rising volume of sisterly love—they were completely impervious to her pleas for them to knock it off—Noelle flipped the van's sun visor down and surveyed the damage in its small mirror. She attempted to smooth her heavy auburn hair and to blot away the feverish heat in her cheeks.

The girls' bickering increased. Great, just great. Even if, by some miracle, the family didn't think they rolled in looking like a complete mess, it would be harder to hide they were a grouchy, broken disaster.

Why did the best things in life always turn out to

be fiction? True love. Happily ever after. Teleportation machines. What Noelle wouldn't give for a Beam me up, Scottie moment. *What.*

Chapter 2

THE OVAL SIGN LOOMED HUGE and unavoidable to their right. "You won't be able to miss it," his younger brother Callum had promised and as usual he was right, Cade thought gloomily. Still, the sign was attractive. To him anyway. He wondered if it was Noelle's taste at all and a familiar leaden weight pushed in on him, making it hard to breath. But how long had it been since he'd had any clue what his wife wanted, what she liked, what would make her happy? Years maybe. Shouldn't he be used to it by now?

As he turned into the long driveway, he slowed the minivan and studied the sign more closely. It was made from carved cedar and featured two mountains topped with glinting tin that looked like snow-topped peaks. A yellow sun rose up behind them. Block letters announced River's Sigh B & B along the bottom. Somehow the effect was both artsy and businesslike. Cade wondered if his mother was behind its creation.

He shot a glance at the girls in the rearview mirror. They were squabbling as usual, but had listened to their mom and straightened their clothing. Eva was pulling her ebony curls—hair that always reminded him of his brother Callum's—into a ponytail. Emily was scrubbing at the orange Slurpee stain that ringed her mouth. When had Noelle gotten so concerned about appearances anyway? He missed the woman who used to decorate with wooden plaques that said things like, "If you've come to see me, welcome. If you've come to see my house, make an appointment!" and who let the kids dress themselves no matter how outlandishly they did it. But she was gone because of him, so what could he really say?

He knew he overcompensated with the kids, was too soft which forced Noelle to be too hard. She was always the bad cop. He wasn't even a cop. But after the battlefield that was his childhood with his dad, all he wanted was to keep the peace. He didn't share every negative thought he had. He didn't get enmeshed in long, pointless conversations about their problems. But instead of harmony in their home, it seemed to create the opposite.

And now they were on "holidays" with her sugges- tion that they separate, made just days earlier, burning a hole in his gut. She'd called it a "trial," but he knew full well, even if she hadn't voiced it out loud, what she really wanted was a divorce. She was just biding her time. He wanted to punch a hole in a fucking wall thinking about it—but, of course, he didn't. He wasn't like his dad. Not in all ways, at least. He could control himself. And he would. Why couldn't Noelle see that?

He was always working so hard to keep things together. *Always.*

"Wow," Noelle said suddenly. "It really is gorgeous here, isn't it?" The awe in her voice was cute and made her sound, for the briefest second, like the woman who used to love him.

The whole van went silent, as they each took in the ancient forest surrounding them. Massive cedars reached for the sky, some of them so big that Cade didn't think the four of them, holding hands, could make a loop around their trunks. Other assorted conifers also crowded in, and random names came back to him. Hemlock. Spruce. Jack Pine. Fir. He was shocked by the variety of needle shapes, colors, and textures. How had he forgotten what a forest looked like? He'd grown up in Greenridge, for crying out loud. A leafy plant with jewel red berries drew his eye to the forest floor and its velvet carpet of gleaming moss.

Cade wasn't an outdoors guy, not really—he spent his time obsessing about room dimensions and floor space—but he found himself wanting to get out of the van and rub some of the bark or touch the moss. He didn't though. Instead he sped up. And then they were there, pulling up in front of a cedar shake home with a huge porch and old-fashioned multi-paned windows.

"Oh, look at the door!" Emily squealed. "I love it!"

Eva agreed with her sister for once, and they chattered on, pointing out log cabins visible here and there through the trees. Cade studied the bright blue door and wondered at it. Why paint it such a glaring, impractical shade? A neutral color would be better, less out there, more appealing to the masses—and Callum was running a business, after all. Maybe it was a gender thing. Maybe the color was the mysterious new wife's idea—this Jo woman his old man couldn't stand. Probably.

The door opened and Callum strode out, one hand raised in greeting, the other linked with the hand of a short woman with wild curls and a welcoming smile.

Cade almost restarted the van and threw it into reverse. This wasn't the place for them. It was too cutesy. Too overtly cozy and cheerful. It would only highlight everything he and Noelle no longer had, everything they weren't. It wouldn't help her see they'd once had something good, something they should try to salvage.

It was too late though. Eva had pushed the release button on the side door, and she and Emily were piling out.

What had he done?

He patted his chest pocket and felt the reassuring outline of the letter folded there. At least he had a back up plan if this one failed, right?

Noelle climbed out of the van just as slowly as he did. Her forehead creased and her wide brown eyes narrowed. The weight on his chest increased. A huge desire to be anywhere but here might be the only thing he and his wife had in common anymore.

Chapter 3

THE KIDS WERE TEARING THROUGH the downstairs rooms like small tornados and every happy squeal was like a slap.

"I'm sorry," Cade said. "I asked Callum for separate rooms. I guess he thought I meant separate from the kids."

He looked as unhappy as she felt and Noelle fought to keep from crying for the second time in like, what, two hours? She'd been longing, no scratch that, she'd been desperately *needing* her own space, hence her suggestion about separating in the first place—so how had she ended up here on a so-called family holiday instead, standing so close to Cade they were practically physically touching, yet further apart emotionally than ever?

Jo's warm greeting rang in her memory like a cruel joke. "I can't wait to get to know you guys better, but first, make yourselves comfy. I think you'll love Chinook, lots of room for the kids, but a private floor for mom and dad."

Her assumption that Cade and Noelle would enjoy

this amazing room that somehow managed to be both rustic and luxurious with its log walls, rough hewn wood floors, huge king size bed decked out in crisp cotton and denim, and deep soaker tub was worse than embarrassing. It made Noelle's chest ache with loss and frustration—and, fine, she'd admit it: fury. Most of the tears she cried these days seemed caused more by impotent anger than sadness—no, she took that back too. There was ample sadness. She'd thought sharing the close confines of the generic hotel last night had been bad, but compared to this it seemed like a reprieve. This was a room for lovers. Not for the opposite of that. Not for . . . them.

Cade was talking again and she grew aware of his words slowly, like someone under water struggling toward the surface.

His voice was gruff. "It's fine. I'll just take Emily's room downstairs. She can stay with you." He exhaled through his nose, and Noelle was reminded of a bull just before it charged. And as usual, whether she spoke or held her tongue, it was like she was waving something red.

"No, it's fine. It's a big bed."

Cade didn't look convinced.

"Besides, it'd be weird if one of the kids happened to mention it to someone."

Cade's gaze seared hers. So for once her husband was actually meeting her eyes, but it only confirmed what she already knew: when he looked at her he didn't like what he saw.

"Yeah, and that'd be the end of the world, right? For anyone to know something real about us."

She didn't know what he meant, or she did, but she was too drained to dwell on it. "I still don't know the real reason you dragged us here, Cade, but please don't make it harder than it already is. Let's just get through it. You can have this big family reunion you have your heart set on, and when we get home, back to the city, I mean, we'll get things sorted."

His shoulders slumped, but his eyes continued to burn. Finally he shrugged. "I'll get the suitcases. Callum said they want to feed us tonight. Dinner's at six."

The big dining room was half full when she entered, and Noelle was pleased she'd insisted on them dressing for dinner, despite Cade and the girls' complaints. It didn't matter that everyone else gathering around the table was slightly more casual than they were. She was bound and determined to never be the shoddily dressed ones at an Archer family event ever again. Then she scanned the room once more and realized Cade's father, Duncan, wasn't even there. Maybe their apparel was overkill after all.

Oh, well.

Suddenly the room fell silent behind her, and Noelle knew without looking that Cade must've finally graced them with his presence. It sounded bitchy when she said it like that—*graced them*—or like she was implying he was arrogant, but she didn't mean the observation either of those ways. He just had that effect on people. They acted *like* he graced them. And she should've been used to it by now, but she never really was. It had occurred to her that this power of Cade's might explain the attraction of Raymond's friendship. He was as uncharismatic and unassuming as could be. But she didn't want to think about Raymond, and how he'd ended up betraying her too. She'd been clear from the start that she was only interested in friendship, and he'd promised that was all he wanted too. Until suddenly, a week ago, when he'd made the stupid declaration that he wanted more. That's what triggered her decision to leave Cade. Not that she wanted Raymond. She did not and had reiterated it. But the idea of using Raymond as an excuse, as a way out of her marriage, was so damned tempting, it shocked her—and made it cuttingly clear that her marriage was really over.

She ignored the well of sorrow and regret that hollowed out her stomach at the notion of ever being with someone other than Cade, of not being with him—and turned to watch the last steps of his entrance, and the group's response to it.

A slip of a girl in a black T-shirt, her hair held up in chopsticks, with a baby on her hip, blushed and grinned then blushed some more when Cade nodded hello.

It was a relief to focus on the next woman's response, a gorgeous blonde, tall and very thin, who gave Cade a full up-down glance. It wasn't, however, followed by the come hither smile Noelle was expecting. Instead the woman turned to Jo and whispered something. Jo shook her head, darted a guilty look at Noelle, and held up a finger to say she'd be a second. "I'm so sorry," she mouthed from across the room. Noelle's curiosity flared. What had the blonde said? What made Jo, up to her armpits in last minute fiddling with a huge tray of appetizers, feel a need to apologize?

Callum was talking with his and Cade's younger brother, Brian. Noelle hadn't seen Brian in ages, but he didn't seem to have changed much. A pretty young redhead with close-cropped hair hung off his arm, looking bored—until her eyes lit on Cade.

Noelle caught a glimpse of herself in a huge mirror hanging on one of the big room's interior walls and sighed. She looked passable, at best.

Two women about Noelle's age giggled, actually *giggled,* when their glances sparked on Cade, and one of them whispered, "I think our stay just got a bit more interesting." The other just kept watching him, unconsciously—or not—twirling a strand of her hair.

Women *and* men always responded in over the top ways to Cade. Part of that, no doubt, was his sheer physical presence. His size and his looks immediately set him apart in a crowd, but it was more than that. He was one of those people who exuded power or something and it subconsciously pulled you toward him, made you feel like if you were in his inner quorum, you'd somehow be special too. In females, this awareness usually manifested in extreme flirting—or equally extreme shyness. Some men also flirted, but most wanted to either join his team or kick his ass. Both desires triggered the same types of behavior: bizarre showmanship spectacles and/or attempts to one up people.

This weird phenomenon used to make Noelle laugh, but that was when she trusted his ability to stay faithful—and her ability to keep her man. Later it had made her nervous and edgy, and prone to keeping a protective hand on his arm to show they were a couple. Still later it just made her irritated. Nowadays she was more immune, kind of looked at it as a weird social science experiment. The human animal was indeed very animal like sometimes.

Cade was shaking hands around the room as Callum made rounds of introductions—and then he was introducing Noelle and the girls, and Noelle got busy doing her own smiling and handshaking.

Noelle could tell the food was delicious from the way everyone at the table ate and ate, but she might as well have been shoveling in straw for all she tasted. The conversation was plentiful and lively—Emily and Eva, still on best behavior, were in constant swivel-mode taking everything in—yet Noelle couldn't think of a single thing to interject. The air conditioning was running full blast and Noelle knew she should be comfortable and relaxed. She was anything but.

All she could see was Jo and Callum's happiness, and the equal and obvious happiness of the tall blonde, introduced as Jo's sister Sam, and her husband Charlie. There was still no hint as to what Sam had whispered when she first laid eyes on Cade, and though Noelle's curiosity lingered, it paled next to the irrational jealousy ripping through her. Sam and Jo. Each still had a sister. Each still had a husband who loved her. Why didn't she? *Why didn't she?*

She forced herself to stop staring at them and switched her focus to something that didn't make her chest seize like she was having a heart attack: Brian's redheaded girlfriend. Yes, much safer. She seemed more engaged than she had earlier, and every so often Brian even looked at her like she might be more than just the flavor of the month.

All in all, it was the cheeriest, most festive meal Noelle had taken part in in months—and it all combined to make her feel like a melting wax farce of a person. Pretty soon she'd be nothing but a puddle of depression and longing.

Come on, Noelle exhorted in her head. It's just three weeks. You can do it.

She felt anything but convinced though, and the minute the main course was finished, she excused herself, begging travel exhaustion, leaving Cade and Eva and Emily to continue the riotous fun.

Chapter 4

CADE TOOK IN NOELLE'S STIFF posture, stilted thank-yous to Jo and Callum, and her awkward "Nice to meet you" and goodnight to everyone else. Only the kiss and squeeze she gave each of the girls seemed genuine and held a trace of what he used to consider her indomitable warmth. She paused at his side and he flinched. Damn it, he actually flinched.

And then, he couldn't believe it, she brushed her lips against his temple. He knew better than to put any stock in the small fire of hope that her nearness kindled. Knew way better. In fact, he couldn't believe she had the fucking nerve. They could hardly exchange two words in private, but in public she'd kiss him? He'd always thought he brought all the problems to their marriage, but now he wondered. Maybe she had more in common with his folks than he'd ever known. She was obsessed with what other people might or might not think. She'd never been like that before, or not that he'd noticed. She'd always seemed the opposite—one of the reasons he'd fallen in love with her in the first place. Had she always been hiding this shallowness, or was it a poison he'd somehow injected into her over the years?

Still, despite how he knew, he deeply *knew*, the kiss was only for the benefit of those around the table, his stomach clenched thinking on it. Later he'd be crawling into bed beside her for the first night in how long? Yesterday, they'd cohabited a hotel room because there weren't two available, but he'd been smart enough not to entertain any delusions of sharing a bed. And he'd been right. Noelle claimed one of the queen size beds for her and Emily, directed Eva to the couch because she didn't like to sleep with her parents anymore, and him to the other bed so he'd "have enough space."

Now Cade thought of the kid free room and Noelle in the bed beside him, imagined the possibility of her butter soft legs accidentally brushing against his, and felt gutted. Absolutely gutted.

"Cade. *Cade*." Callum, a little loud, almost alarmed, brought Cade back to the here and now.

"Yeah?"

"Are you all right?"

Cade looked around, surprised. When had everyone left the table? The young mom—Aisha, he thought her name was—who was clearing the dessert dishes, the baby at her feet, and he and Callum were the only people in the room.

His face must've shown his next question because Callum said, "Outside playing Bocce. Don't worry. Jo will take care of the kids. Now, seriously, are you okay?"

"Sure. Of course. Why?"

Callum's eyebrow quirked and though he didn't say a word, his face yelled bullshit loud and clear.

"I've just got a lot on my mind. That's why I'm looking forward to helping you on that cabin like we talked about. Hard work's exactly what I need."

"You were serious about that?"

A terrible possibility occurred to Cade. "You weren't just having me on, were you? You are renovating another cabin?"

"Well, yeah, I planned to. We were in a hurry to get the place open, so we hired a crew to get the first five cabins up to snuff, but I don't want to let other guys have all the fun."

"Oh, good. That's that." Cade lumbered to his feet, then realized Callum was holding something back. "What? Just because I work with design software more often than not these days doesn't mean I've forgotten how to bang nails. I won't get in your way."

"It's not that—well, it's kind of that." Callum grinned, but it faded fast. "It's more like I don't understand why. If I was surprised when you called and said you wanted to stay a month, I'm stunned that you want to spend it working on one of my shacks. What's up with you?"

Cade scrubbed his hands over his face. Not only were they not a touchy-feely family, they weren't a talky family. *But you're trying to change that, right, buddy?*

"I, uh, well ... me and Noelle ... we need a change."

Callum just stared.

"So, you know, I figured some time away from the city might do us good."

A swinging door banged open and Aisha, who had disappeared into the kitchen, reappeared with a damp rag in hand.

Callum appeared to be waiting for more clarification, but when Cade didn't add anything, he sighed. "So you guys need ... a change ... and you're going to work on a cabin with me all day, every day?"

"Yeah. Exactly." Cade nodded, relief flooding through him.

This time it was Callum who scrubbed at his face with his hands. "Okay then." He shook his head. "I'll see you bright and early tomorrow morning."

Chapter 5

NOELLE AWOKE IN THE HUGE bed, the whirring fan her only company. Its cool caress stirred the solitary sheet that half covered her torso and kissed her bare legs. She did a covert search of the room, saw she was alone, and stretched luxuriously.

Had Cade come to bed at all? she wondered—then remembered waking in the night and seeing him hugging the left hand side of the bed in deep sleep. An indent in the pillow beside her confirmed her memory as reality. So he was already up and gone. That was a good thing, right? Her skin warmed. She'd had the strangest dreams, as if her body had responded to the very presence of Cade, however far apart they lay, triggering her mind to replay every one of their hottest moments. And in sleep, all her disappointments and hurt were far away. She was happy to know her body could still enjoy the thought of sex, at least, and hoped the object of her fantasies wouldn't always be Cade Archer.

At that thought, and becoming aware of the scent of rich dark coffee wafting up the stairs, the lovely, languid feeling of sensuality she'd woken with fell away.

She stood and walked to the huge window. The view was almost unbelievable. In the distance, huge navy mountains with gray craggy tips stretched into the bluest sky she'd ever seen. Closer in, sheltering a dancing creek, rows of evergreen trees stood sentry, so brilliant in the early morning sun they glinted and glowed like each limb was decked out in emeralds. Jewel-bright orange, scarlet and yellow Nasturtium blossoms with huge round jade-green leaves spilled from half-barrel planters. She opened the big window and leaned out, pulling air into her lungs. So fresh. So good. And she made a decision.

Cade, for whatever insane undisclosed reason, wanted them to spend time here before they took a break from their marriage? Well, fine. She'd do her best to enjoy herself—and to make sure Eva and Emily did too. She was not going to be the bad guy in this scenario, the grouch who wrecked their last family holiday. After all, who knew when they'd have a chance for this type of vacation again? Cade definitely wouldn't let her starve or have the kids go without once they split, but she wasn't planning on living extravagantly off him. Until she figured out what she was going to do for work, it would be back to living simply for a while. She wondered, just for a moment, if maybe that was Cade's motivation. Maybe he wanted to remind her how much she'd be giving up in terms of ease and luxury. But she'd already thought about that and she was done going without all the things money couldn't buy. It was too soul destroying. Not to mention, a terrible example for her daughters.

A small knock sounded on the bedroom door.

"Yes, hello?"

"Mom?"

Noelle sighed in relief that it wasn't Cade and stepped back from the window. "Come on in."

Eva and Emily traipsed into the room, wearing sundresses and identical grins. Noelle noticed they'd already brushed their hair, too. Eva's shining black curls were held back with a purple headband. Emily's russet hair, so like her own, was pulled back in a slightly bumpy ponytail, but she'd obviously tried hard.

"You guys are up so early and you're dressed so pretty. What's the occasion?"

Emily whipped out the hand she'd held behind her back to reveal a bouquet of cheery wildflowers in small vase.

Eva disappeared outside the door and there was a slight scuffling as something was lifted from the floor. She reappeared with a wicker breakfast tray, bearing bacon, a bowl of mixed fruit, a tiny jug of cream and a whole carafe of coffee.

"We had breakfast with Daddy because it's a bed-and-breakfast, so they'll always feed us breakfast if we're up in time, but we have to make our own lunch and dinner and—"

"Dad said it would be a nice treat if we brought you breakfast in bed," Eva said, cutting Emily off impatiently. Emily didn't seem perturbed so Noelle let the rudeness slide. "And Auntie Jo agreed, so here you are."

"Well, thank you very much. It looks delicious." Noelle settled back into the bed.

"You could get used to this, right, Mom?" Emily said and they all giggled at the old joke. *I could get used to this* was what they'd always said whenever something particularly nice happened, but hearing it now, Noelle realized it had been a long time since any of them uttered it. The thought made her sad.

"Okay, we'll leave you in peace and quiet to enjoy your coffee. We'll be downstairs if you need us."

"Or on the lawn playing with the dogs. Auntie Jo and Auntie Sam—"

"Sam isn't our aunt."

"It doesn't matter. I can call her aunt if I want to. She said. And *anyway*, I'm talking to *Mom*. They both have dogs, Mom. And we can play with them whenever we want because they love everyone."

Noelle shook her head, smiling as the kids left the room, so intent on nattering at each other they'd basically forgotten her. She was halfway through her meal when something occurred to her that practically curdled the coffee she'd been enjoying.

Dad said it would be a nice treat.

We'll leave you in peace and quiet to enjoy your coffee.

Those weren't phrases the kids would come up with on their own. They were quoting Cade. And since when did he want to do anything nice for her or even think twice about how her mornings went? She had a sickening feeling that she knew exactly why he'd wanted this blasted holiday. It wasn't a chance to have one special vacation with the girls—hence, why he wasn't even hanging out with them on their very first day there. He wasn't going to quietly agree to a separation the way he said he would. He was going to try to manipulate her into forgetting the whole thing by making her feel too guilty to leave him. Well, it wasn't going to work. He could be as sweet and conciliatory as he wanted. She wouldn't be fooled. What was the expression? Fool me once, shame on you. Fool me twice, shame on me.

No, she wasn't going to be fooled again.

Noelle showered quickly, then slathered herself in some chemical laden oil-free moisturizer that was supposed to keep wrinkles and shine at bay, knowing it was futile. As soon as she hit the outdoors, her whole body would be slick with sweat. She pinned her hair up. That would be cooler at least. Then, with a mixture of irritation and regret, she wiggled into her torture device. The ten (twenty!) pounds she'd gained and hadn't managed to lose definitely looked less sloppy with a control top onesie, even if wearing it did make her a hodgepodge combo of homicidal and melancholy.

The girls cheered when she said she was going to take them into town to grocery shop and pick out a treat or two.

Jo, however, looked surprised. "But we don't mind you eating with us. We want you to. You're not formal guests. You're family."

"That's sweet, Jo, thank you, but three weeks is a long time. You'll be feeding us breakfasts. We don't want to impose."

"It's no imposition. I promise."

"We'll see. Thanks though," Noelle said again.

Hurt flickered in Jo's friendly eyes, but she rallied quickly. "I'm sorry. I can be overly enthusiastic about things. It's a curse. You're probably looking forward to alone time with Cade and the girls before everyone else arrives."

"Yes," Noelle agreed. "It's just they're growing so quickly and days go so fast."

Jo nodded and apologized again, which was just nuts. The woman didn't have anything to apologize for. Noelle hated that needing to keep her guard up around Cade's family meant that perfectly nice seeming Jo might feel like she was getting the cold shoulder, but it couldn't be helped.

Noelle was about to leave when Jo's voice stopped her by the door. "Just one more thing. Would you consider taking part in a girls' night sometime in the next week or two? Mr. Archer, I mean, Duncan, is planning a stag night and he wants Caren to do something too."

"A stag night? Are you kidding me?" Noelle exclaimed, completely forgetting to keep her voice modulated and her demeanor calm.

Jo looked shocked, then grinned. "That's exactly what I said! I guess Duncan thinks it's appropriate because they're renewing their vows. He wants the whole procedure to mimic their original wedding. I think it makes a stag night even stranger. The old creep just wants to—" Jo broke off abruptly. Her eyes widened in embarrassed horror. "I mean . . ."

"No excuses or apologies needed. He *is* an old creep, but I'll deny it to my grave if you tell anyone I said so."

Jo laughed, a merry, sincere sound that made Noelle like her even more, despite her resolve to keep Cade's family at arm's length. "Deal. And ditto."

"And regarding girls' night, I'll think about it," Noelle promised, and she would, if only because Jo seemed sincerely nice and Noelle couldn't imagine what special hell it must be living in the same town with Caren and Duncan.

And then the conversation and tentative plan faded from her mind. She made an obligatory call to Cade's parents, was beyond grateful to get the machine, and left a message saying she'd be happy (lie!) to get together for some special grandparent/grandkid time, then gathered up the girls and headed to town.

When they got back to Chinook cabin that evening, she and the girls were exhausted from going hard all day in the heat. Air conditioning appeared to be an optional feature in Greenridge's stores and restaurants, and while cool by comparison to the outdoor temperatures, the solitary mall and cute downtown core of independent shops weren't the refreshing oasis she'd hoped for. Sweat was literally running down her back as she brought in the groceries, and she knew her carefully arranged updo was a limp mess. Oh, well—at least she'd had the foresight to know she wouldn't want to cook.

The girls were outside wading in the creek behind the cabin (Noelle had double-checked with Jo that it was safe, then triple-checked it herself, making sure it wasn't too deep or flowing too fast.), and she'd just tossed a salad and placed a deli-roasted chicken and some bakeshop rolls on the table when Cade walked in. He was dusty, his hair was curling from the humidity, and his skin seemed darker already, making his blue eyes all the bluer—but other than that, the man seemed impervious to the heat, despite working in it all day, damn him anyway.

"You made dinner?" he asked, sounding pleased.

"Of course. I always do, don't I?" She hadn't meant to be so snappish, but honestly, he acted like it was some big novel thing that she had food ready.

He sighed. "Do I have time for a shower before we

eat?"

She shrugged. He looked uncertain, then said, "I'll be fast," and disappeared up the stairs.

As she watched him go, she realized he was wearing pants she'd never seen before, some sort of tough, super heavy-duty denim in a rusty brown color. They looked totally hot. Even making the observation in her own head, she blushed. "I meant temperature wise," she muttered, feeling like a big idiot. "*Temperature* wise." But her inner self wasn't fooled one bit.

"What?" Cade called back down the stairs. "Are you talking to me?"

Sure, pick this moment to actually hear something I've said, she thought. "No," she hollered back. "But please hurry. I want to feed the kids and get them to bed."

Not a word came back in reply and long minutes later the shower turned on. Noelle was one hundred percent certain Cade had stood naked by the tub, intentionally stalling, just to spite her. Not that she entirely blamed him. When exactly had she become such a big bitch? Ah, who was she kidding? She knew when. Could trace it to the exact date and time practically. It was like her heart had shriveled that night and had never fully recovered. But what could she do about it? Nothing at all—or so the passage of time suggested anyway.

She found a round-bellied glass jug in a cabinet and made lemonade, throwing in two trays of ice cubes. Then she went outside to fetch the girls, the heat hitting her with a full-body smack the minute she opened the door. Miracle of miracles, they didn't complain too much about getting out of the creek. Emily's teeth were actually chattering, which seemed hilarious considering.

"The water is so cold, Mom. It's like liquid snow."

"Because it is sort of. It stays freezing cold all year because it's glacier fed or something. Or I think that's what Auntie Jo said," Eva informed them both.

Well, Auntie Jo was sure a fountain of knowledge, wasn't she? Noelle bit back the bitter thoughts. Tried to focus on the fact that it was nice Jo fielded her nieces' questions and didn't seem burdened by them. More than nice. It was great.

Back inside Chinook, the girls washed up and sprinted for the table. Cade was already seated.

"Okay, dig in," Noelle said.

"We're all at the table together. That's rare, hey?" Emily announced with her childlike way of stating the uncomfortable and the obvious. "Are we going to pray?"

It used to be something they did before every meal, but it had been a while since Noelle had felt like it. There were some things she didn't mind putting a good front on, but prayer wasn't one of them. It should be genuine or not at all. Still, what else could she say to her sweet youngest daughter except yes? From Emily, any words of gratitude or supplication would be sincere.

"That'd be lovely, Em. Would you do the honors?"

Emily thanked God for the beautiful sunshine, for their family and that they got to eat together, and for the "beautiful, beautiful, so nice and so friendly, perfect pet dogs," and asked to have just as nice a day tomorrow.

"Amen," Noelle, Cade and Eva echoed when she finished.

Noelle served them each salad and Cade divvied out chicken. "That was a nice prayer, sweetie," Noelle said, more to fill the stilted quiet than out of any desire to converse. "And it's wonderful that you're having fun with the dogs, but don't get any ideas. 'Perfect' pets or not, we aren't getting a dog."

"Well, never say never," Cade interjected, pouring lemonade into his and Emily's glasses, then passing the pitcher to Eva.

Noelle shot Cade a dark shut-up-right-now look. He was totally oblivious, or was he? Maybe he was being passive-aggressive, showing her that if they split, the girls would get a dog if they lived with him.

"Yeah, never say never," Emily chimed in.

Eva looked from her mom to her dad and grabbed a bun. "Can I get my book?"

Reading at the table was Eva's new thing, and while Noelle felt guilty about it, she didn't blame her for wanting to escape and usually let her.

"Not tonight, Eva, sorry," Noelle said. "And you're

right, Emily. Never say never."

A delighted pre-victory squeal poured forth from Emily.

"When you're a grown-up, you can have as many pets as you want."

"Or maybe before, if Daddy says. Right, Daddy?"

Noelle clamped her jaw shut so tightly her molars ground together. In his defense—except she really didn't want to defend him—Cade looked stunned. He didn't dart a look at Emily; instead his eyes sought Noelle's and he shook his head lightly. She glanced away. His next words only confused her further. Or maybe *shocked* would be more accurate.

"I'm sorry, baby girl. I just meant sometime in your life you could probably get a dog, not now. I'm not going against Mom's wishes. We make decisions together."

"You do?" Emily asked innocently. "When?"

Eva's bun had been buttered and was gone. She reached for another. "May I *please* get my book?"

"Yeah, yeah, sure," Noelle said distractedly.

"I thought you told her no."

Noelle studied Cade and he met her look, but his eyes gave nothing away. What was he playing at? His sudden siding with her wasn't going to make her instantly forgive everything from the past, and if he was going to call her out every time she told the kids one thing then waffled out of exhaustion, she'd go crazier than she already felt.

"No book, kiddo," Cade said. "Like Mom already said. We'll visit while we eat. You can read before bed."

Eva nodded and took a bite of chicken. While No-elle appreciated it whenever her eldest obeyed without a series of whines or complaints, she wished that it wasn't always Cade who got the deferential obedience, that she wasn't always the one who got argued with.

"So what did you guys do today?" Cade asked after a mouthful or two and dead silence.

Eva shrugged. "A lot of stuff."

Emily bounced in her chair in agreement. "Yeah, *a lot*." She proceeded to list each activity, starting with going to the dining hall for breakfast with Cade and Eva and bringing back food for Noelle.

Cade listened patiently. "Wow, sounds fun," he said when she finished with a flourish.

"And did you enjoy your morning?" he added. It took Noelle a second to realize he was talking to her. She finished swallowing, and looked at him.

"Well, yes . . ."

"That sounds hesitant."

She shrugged. "I guess I'm just confused. Why did you do that anyway?"

"Do what?"

"Get the girls to bring me breakfast? I'm perfectly capable of making toast in the morning or going without food until lunchtime."

Cade pinched the bridge of his nose and sighed. "I

don't know. I thought it would be nice."

"I don't believe you."

"I think she did think it was nice," Eva interjected, then looked confused. "Or she did earlier anyway."

"Come on," Cade said a bit imploringly. "Not everything I do or say has a hidden agenda."

"Yes, it does." Noelle stood up, turned away from Cade, and gathered and stacked the dinner plates.

"Hey," Emily complained. "I wanted to chew on that bone still. I'm pretending I'm a dog."

"You're such a baby," Eva whispered ferociously.

"You can be a dog who eats a Popsicle if you want," Noelle said.

"Yay!" Emily skipped toward the fridge and opened the freezer compartment.

"You're unbelievable," Cade muttered.

Noelle's heart raced and she felt like she might explode with rage and the huge unfairness of it all.

"Mom," Eva's voice now, quiet but insistent at her shoulder. "Can I *please* read my book with my dessert if I sit on the porch?"

"Yes, fine, great," Noelle said in one whooshing exhale.

Eva didn't waste time, lest her other parental unit withdraw permission again, and joined her younger sibling rummaging in the freezer compartment. Noelle was only peripherally aware of the girls still hovering around the borders of the room when Cade spoke again, his voice as cold as hers had been.

"Maybe this whole trip was a mistake," he said.

"You think?" she replied, making her tone just as mean, even while she wished they had contained themselves one more second until the girls were on the porch, out of hearing range.

Cade stormed out to who knew where, and Noelle quickly did up the few plates, prodded the girls to shower and brush their teeth, then tucked them in. He still hadn't shown up when she climbed into bed, nor had he appeared by the time she finished two chapters of a book heralded as a "side splitting laugh riot" that hadn't made her smile once yet.

As had become her new bedtime ritual, she spent a few minutes pointlessly rehashing the past. Had Cade ever been able to honestly share anything that went on in his head? Had she? And if they'd somehow managed to communicate differently, would they still be in the mess they were in? But shoulda, woulda, coulda. Maybe it didn't matter. Whatever their communication failures were, it was all water under a long past, and now burned, bridge. And being willing to shoulder some of the blame for their marriage's collapse aside, there were some actions that had no excuse. That there was no coming back from.

She cried herself to sleep, despite her best attempts not to, and if Cade crawled in beside her at any point during the night, he was stealthy and kept a good distance. She didn't hear or sense him once.

Chapter 6

CADE SAT IN THE ARMCHAIR in the corner of the room, waiting for dawn. In about an hour he could appear at Callum's door, without it being too pathetic or obvious that something was messed up in Chinook cabin. What kind of guy wanted to work every day as long and as hard as possible when he was on holidays with his wife and kids, if he was any kind of a husband and father? The answer was pretty clear. No kind of husband and father at all. So, in a nutshell, *him*.

The sheer curtains in front of the open window shuddered in a small breeze—a breeze that would no doubt die as soon as the sun rose. Noelle had long ago kicked off all the covers, even the sheet. She wore nothing but a shortie nightie—a testament, if anyone needed one, of just how hot this summer was. How long had it been since he'd seen that much of her? He didn't understand why she covered herself up so thoroughly and wore such old lady clothes these days. Was she trying to reinforce her "Stay the hell away from me" message? She didn't need to. He got it loud and clear from her body language. And really, he knew what was under her clothes. She could wear any tent she wanted; it didn't disguise what he was missing out on. No, he knew his loss full and well—and baking in the sun all day did nothing to quell his desire for her, like he'd hoped it would.

The curtains fluttered more energetically, and as if feeling the light wind on her skin and liking it, Noelle opened her limbs wide, stretching in a big X across the bed. Her shortie nightie really was *short*.

Damn.

He forced himself to look away and fought the voice in his head that whispered, You're her husband. Your place is in bed beside her. You want her. What's the problem?

The problem was that while Cade was, of course, yes, her husband and he believed the second line and definitely agreed with the third, he wasn't the kind of guy to assume anything or push anything on anyone, especially on his wife. What he wanted was for her to want him again. Maybe if she hadn't made it abundant-ly clear a few months ago—by stating it out loud—that sex was off the table for them, he would've given into the temptation, risked her wrath, and seen if he could rouse her interest. He smiled at the thought. He was fully confident of his ability to do that. Noelle loved sex. So why was she so dead set against him touching her? They'd argued and fought over a billion things over their eleven-year marriage and twelve-year relationship. Sex—really good, amazing sex—was always the thing that brought them back together. It was the one way he could show her exactly how much he loved her, how much she consumed him.

You know full well why that doesn't work anymore, a different voice said. He sighed, clenched his fists, and let his eyes fall back on Noelle's sleeping form. She didn't love him anymore. That's why she wouldn't touch him or let him touch her. And that's what he deserved.

He thought about dinner, how his plan for family togetherness had totally bombed, and his response to Noelle, the way he'd been instantly angered by her anger. He knew exactly what sat between them, what lay behind her sniping comments about nonsense. His guilt and fury at himself for wrecking them rushed out against his will sometimes, always mistargeted. It seemed like he was angry with Noelle, but really he was furious, always, in every way, at himself.

Noelle mumbled under her breath and sighed softly, sounding content and at peace—something she never was when she was awake anymore. Then she rolled over, hugging a pillow close.

Cade bit his lip and pressed his fists into his eyes. He had to make her see, had to get her to give him another chance. If he could just work hard enough for her and the girls on family related things, it was bound to show her where his priorities lay: on her and the girls. On reestablishing and maintaining family life, their own and their extended. He knew how much she'd lost moving to the west coast, away from her eastern roots—and how it had torn her apart when Melissa died—and how worse than useless he'd been at helping with her grief. If he could pull it off, she'd not only see fit to give him a chance, but maybe she'd build relationships with some of his siblings that could help fill the void. He hoped anyway.

He patted the pocket of his shirt for his if-all-else-failed letter. It was a comforting presence. Then he glanced at his phone in the brightening room. Five thirty a.m. Still pretty early, but he couldn't hang out there another minute like a sad, impotent weirdo.

Before he left the room, he paused by her side of the bed.

"I'm going to work, babe. I'll see you when I get back. I love you." His words were as quiet as the gauzy movement of fabric at the window.

Noelle mumbled incoherently again and buried her face deep in the pillow, but it made him smile nonetheless. It was almost like she'd responded to him.

Chapter 7

ONCE MORE CADE WAS UP and gone long before Noelle awoke. For the second day in a row, she, Emily and Eva went sightseeing around Greenridge, this time taking in some heritage sites and parks—again with a serious air conditioning deficiency.

She didn't see or hear from Caren or Duncan, even though she'd left another message, so felt no guilt about the in-law free gallivant. That evening she made another simple meal for her and the girls, got them off to bed, then stuck a note on the cabin door asking Cade to come in quietly and fend for himself for dinner if he hadn't already eaten. She tried and failed not to wonder where he was, seeing he'd left at dawn and now it was dusk. They might as well have stayed home, for how similar his way of "spending family time together" was.

On the third morning, she'd assumed she and the girls would echo the previous days—but no, everything changed.

Cade was long gone when her eyes opened. That part was the same. But the girls balked at the notion of getting into the van and seeing anything else.

"We've been to every store already and I don't like shopping anyway," Eva groaned.

"I did like the olden days park thing and the library and the mall, and I do want to go to the lake the lady at the ice-cream store told us about, but not today. I want to play here. It's so nice, Mommy, and we've hardly seen any of it." Emily's voice was half-cajole, half-whine.

"Isn't it too hot to run around outside?"

Both girls looked at her like she was crazy.

"It's summer, Mom. It's supposed to be hot," Eva said.

"And Auntie Jo wants to see more of us, I promise. She even said we would never be in her way."

Great. So Emily had repeated Noelle's excuse to Jo—and then Jo had been burdened with having to be polite to them. Awesome.

"Can we please stay here to explore, please, pretty please?" The girls begged as one, obviously a pre-planned strategy. Oh well, at least they weren't fighting with each other.

Noelle took in their exaggeratedly wide-eyed, imploring expressions and knew she was beat. She grinned and shook her head. "Okay, okay. Make sure you ask Auntie Jo if there's anything you can help her with first though, and stay away from anything she says to steer clear of."

The girls shrieked in agreement and darted out.

Noelle wished she had one ounce of their energy.

She meandered around the cabin, tidying, then read for a while, checking for the girls every so often by going to the porch and listening for their voices. The air that blasted her when she opened the door was furnace-like. Was this how she was going to spend her summer? In self-imposed exile? No, she decided. Absolutely not. She'd do one task related to planning for her next phase of life per day, but then it was out of the cabin for her, too. She couldn't imagine having fun here under the circumstances, but it would be good practice for moving on: doing things despite a lack of passion or desire. Hopefully, in time, zest for something would return.

She entered a to-do list into her cell phone, and considered that her job for the day. She checked her Facebook messages, read the latest one from Raymond, sighed heavily and turned off her phone without responding. There was nothing to say, after all.

Then, after retouching her sweating make up and drinking a massive glass of water in a desperate attempt to hydrate herself, she decided to heed her own advice and see if Jo needed anything. She had to be feeling overwhelmed in this heat, planning food and festivities for a hundred people for a three-day event, even if it was weeks away.

Jo wasn't in the communal dining room or the office, and Noelle glanced at her phone to check the time, remembering that after one o'clock Callum and

Jo were pretty much off duty. Sure enough, it was quarter after one. She contemplated knocking on their home's bright blue door, but just then a voice piped up behind her. "Can I help you?"

Noelle turned to see the young mom, Jo's niece. She remembered the girl's name at the last minute. *Aisha.* "No, it's all right. I was just looking for Jo."

"Well, it's your lucky day." Aisha pointed. Jo was walking over from her old pickup truck, carrying two large, very full reusable grocery bags.

"Hey, Jo," Noelle said, feeling stupidly shy. "Is there something I can help with today? The girls have had enough mother-daughter time."

"Yeah, I thought it looked like they'd shifted to dog-kid time pretty devotedly."

Noelle followed Jo's gaze and her eyes crinkled at the sight of the girls splashing through a sprinkler, followed by a slim German shepherd and a wiry mutt of some kind. Both dogs were soaked and bedraggled—and undeniably happy looking. She didn't even care that the girls hadn't changed into swimsuits. In this heat, they'd be dry ten minutes after hopping out of the spray. "They're not in your way, are they?"

"Not in the least, and I'll just boss them around if they are, don't worry."

Noelle nodded. "So anything I can do?"

"Well, if you really don't mind . . . Shopping took longer than planned and I'm trying a new recipe I need to get a start on, but I also wanted to bring something cool for the poor guys pounding nails in this sun."

Noelle nodded, not fully understanding what Jo was asking, and followed her into the kitchen.

"If you could make a big pitcher of iced tea while I throw together some sandwiches, then take it all to Callum and Cade, I'd appreciate it."

It wasn't like Noelle could say no or anything, so after a pause that was one beat too long, she forced a smile. "Of course. And let me make the sandwiches too. Just point me to the ingredients."

As Noelle assembled, Jo worked beside her in a flurry of chopping and dicing, making small talk about how Eva and Emily reminded her of herself and Sam when they were young. "Do you have sisters?" Jo asked.

Noelle's heart pounded. She didn't want to have to put things in the past tense or to have to explain anything. "One. Melissa. She was just a year younger than me." She rushed on. "And I have two brothers. They, everyone, they all live on the other side of the country."

Jo looked a bit odd. "That must be . . . so hard."

"Not so much anymore," Noelle said briskly. "I'm kind of used to it now."

Jo continued to watch her, then gave a single nod and got back to work.

Soon Noelle had a tray stocked with plump egg salad sandwiches on fresh baked bread, a bowl of crunchy dill pickles, veggie sticks and dip, and homemade peanut butter fudge bars for dessert.

"Do you always make Callum lunches like this?" Noelle asked as she put sprigs of just-picked mint into the iced tea as directed by Jo.

Jo looked up from some herbs she was mincing. "Well, yes, I guess—but you should see some of the meals he makes me." Her tone seemed almost apologetic. "We're both in the kitchen a lot, both love to cook and make homemade things. And it's not that labor intensive, honestly. The eggs were leftover from breakfast."

"Newlyweds," Noelle announced—or maybe snorted, she admitted—as she grabbed napkins.

Jo froze for a second, but when she spoke her voice was casual. "I guess," she said again. "But I don't know. I hope doing nice things for each other lasts. I want it to. We waited a long time to finally be together."

And Noelle suddenly remembered that was true. Cade had made the tiniest comment about his lawyer brother turned baker and B & B owner when Callum announced his surprising marriage via e-mail a year or so earlier.

"Well, look at that," Cade had said. "Everything works out for that little bastard. He even gets to marry the high school sweetheart he never stopped pining for."

Noelle had been a little hurt because back then she was still in denial mode, thinking she and Cade were basically happy and, to quote his own words, had everything working out for them, too.

"I'm sorry, Jo," Noelle said. "I didn't mean to sound snide. I'm really happy for you guys. Truly."

Jo shrugged and when she spoke, Noelle had the distinct impression she was holding back. "Thank you. I do feel very blessed."

Must be nice, Noelle thought, but for once she wasn't feeling bitter or snarky. Just sad. She remembered all too well when she'd felt blessed too. So when had what she and Cade enjoyed so much started to fall apart? And why? Was it all the hours Cade worked? Was it her grief over her sister and how she hadn't been able to articulate how she felt, so she closed herself off, hoping that by not talking about it the pain would eventually just go away? Was that what triggered the last straw, his unfaithfulness? Or had the roots of their problems always been present? Maybe the causes she clung to were actually the product of pre-existing issues. When had they stopped doing nice things for each other, starting living alone though they shared the same house?

"So you're all set. Do you know where to find them?" Jo asked, interrupting Noelle's limp down More-regrets Lane.

"I think so."

Jo led her out to the wide porch and pointed. "There's a path that links the five rentable cabins together. It breaks into a Y just past Chinook, that's your cabin, and takes you to another group of three buildings that are, well, let's just call them works in progress, shall we? Follow the sound of hammering and eighties' music and you shouldn't have a problem."

Noelle laughed, despite how awkward it would be to bring Cade lunch when they hadn't so much as laid eyes on each other since their stupid dinner fight.

She found the path no problem and suspected the work site wasn't far away, but she kept getting distracted. Jo had beautiful flowerbeds in front of each cabin and in the center of the property. Was she aware of the overgrown perennial beds in the back here? There were at least three varieties of lavender, standing knee high in the equally tall wild grasses. And there were rhododendrons looking stifled and squashed by some prickly horror plant. What was it called again? Oh, right—devil's club. Assorted clumps of daisies, peonies, and lilies struggled, as well. The later were well past their blooming season, but their greenery would be eye-catching on its own if they were weeded. It looked like the bed ran along the whole path, though nature was doing its best to overtake it. It was a shame it was so let go, but then again, maybe Jo intended to get to it later. The work to be done around River's Sigh must feel staggering at times.

Noelle remained stationary, surveying her surroundings, for a long time. It had been a while since she'd dug around in a garden. Her own beds at home were pristine, well-ordered and manicured—and tended by a hired landscaper because early in their marriage, when they still visited Cade's family semi-regularly, she'd heard Cade's dad complain about how his wife always had paint on her hands and looked like a laborer. Noelle internalized the lesson. She wouldn't let her passion for dirt wreck her nails, give her callus-es, and cause her husband embarrassment at work functions.

Now she was surprised by the yearning and inspi-ration the neglected plants sprouted within her. It might even be worth the bug bites and discomfort of kneeling and pulling weeds in a torture-girdle. She'd have to think about it.

She shifted and the ice in the sweating pitcher of cold tea tinkled and brought her back to the task at hand. Lunch. For Callum and Cade. Right. She walked more quickly than she had been, and the platter of food and drinks in her hands grew heavier and heavier, as did her unease. Which was nuts. It was only Cade, for crying out loud. They were like oil and water these days, yes, but it wasn't like he'd say anything hurtful or be rude in front of his brother. He'd most likely just ignore her. Which would sting the most. The realiza-tion shocked her a bit.

She didn't hear music or hammering like Jo sug-gested she would. Just voices, low and intense. If the girls were with her or she'd made more noise as she walked, she might not have even noticed Cade and

Callum were talking until she rounded the corner of a weather beaten building almost hidden from sight by a large, bushy cedar hedge. A rickety gray sawhorse sat by a rough, splintery wall. She tested the sawhorse for sturdiness—it seemed all right—and set the tray down. Then she took a deep breath and tugged at her hemline. Every stupid outfit she had rode up on her thighs in this heat. Attractive. She was about to pick the tray up again and announce lunchtime when she heard her name out of Callum's mouth of all things, not her husband's. She stopped dead in her tracks to listen.

"It's not just you," Callum was saying. "Noelle seems different too."

A gusty exhale was Cade's only response for a long moment, and Noelle figured they were finished their discussion and she'd never know what it was about.

Then Cade spoke, his low voice anger-tinged as it so often was these days. "It's me. I messed everything up."

"What did you do?"

Noelle thought it was interesting that Cade's own brother didn't offer words of consolation or encouragement, like "I'm sure it's not so bad" or something. He seemed to immediately assume that Cade had indeed screwed up. There was a dull thump, like something heavy and metal thudding against wood.

"Nothing."

"So you messed up 'everything' by doing nothing?

Yeah, right."

Noelle bit down on her lip to contain her own rage and hurt. *Nothing*? He called it *nothing*?

"Well, not nothing exactly. It's just . . . complicated."

Another pause. Noelle didn't know if Cade made some gesture or gave some clue with his body language, but all of a sudden there was an explosive rustle like one of the guys jumped to his feet, then Callum practically snarled, "Are you kidding me? You cheated on her, didn't you?"

Noelle's breath caught in her throat, choking her, as she waited for Cade's reply. Would he admit it to his brother? What would his excuse be?

There was a soft, rhythmic slapping sound and Noelle knew Cade was punching his fist lightly into his palm over and over again, his go to movement whenever he was stressed. It was one of the hardest parts of being married for so long and having it all fall apart: how well you knew the other person in some ways, when in other ways you obviously didn't know them at all.

She inhaled and tried to steady her shaking hands. Would Cade lie or tell the truth? Would he give a clue about what Noelle had done, how she'd failed, why he'd been driven to—

"I didn't cheat on her per se."

What the hell? The unkind sun had nothing on the temperature raging through Noelle. She was blinded by white fury. He wouldn't even be honest with himself when he was with his own brother.

"*Per se*? What kind of wording is that? Per se sounds *exactly* like you cheated and you're trying to justify it or talk around it the same way Dad—"

"Don't finish that thought, Callum. I'm warning you. I'll beat the shit out of you."

There was a long minute of absolute silence. Tendrils of hostility and barely constrained animosity snaked around the corner of the house and grabbed hold of Noelle.

"You're the one who brought it up, and if you don't want to be compared to the old man, maybe you shouldn't follow in every one of his damn footsteps."

Cade's voice was strangled. "I said not to—"

Callum interrupted with a humorless, barking laugh. "And maybe it's time *I* say something. You don't call all the shots anymore, big bro. You can probably still beat the crap out of me. Go for it. It won't change anything. If anything, you'll just prove my point."

Noelle pressed a clenched fist to her mouth and bit her knuckles. In spite of everything, she wanted to rush around the corner and challenge Callum's words. Cade wasn't like his father, or not in all the most awful ways anyway, and being constantly compared to that man was probably the single most damaging thing Cade's whole rotten family had ever done to him. And if he'd been a bully to his brothers when he was young, it probably went both ways. It had with her and her siblings—and did with Eva and Emily. Cade wasn't a violent guy. He wasn't.

Noelle felt sure Cade shrugged or something. "Of course I wouldn't actually hit you, you idiot. We're not nine and eleven anymore."

Callum snorted and this time there was trace of humor in it—and acceptance of Cade's unvoiced apology.

"And I . . . it wasn't like mom and dad. It wasn't. It was one time. One stupid, drunken idiot moment. I didn't even sleep with the woman."

Noelle started. What? He hadn't? No . . . he was lying again. He had. Of course he had—or why were they going through all this shit?

"But it was close enough, too close. It might as well have been the same thing."

There was a huffing sound of disbelief or derision and Callum spoke again. "Except, and I can't believe I'm saying this, if you didn't actually screw someone else, *you didn't actually screw someone else.* Whatever you did, however bad, maybe you guys can get over it."

"She doesn't know."

"Doesn't know you almost cheated?"

"No, doesn't know I didn't sleep with Sherry."

Sherry. Even hearing her name again made Noelle want to vomit. Every nerve in her body shrieked like she'd been dragged naked over cement behind a truck or something. She sagged against the wall behind her. Felt an itchy shard prick her leg. Noted, stupidly, that the ice in the pitcher was melting quickly even though it was in the shade. She was supposed to be feeding them lunch. Instead she was . . . being cut in half. Was Cade serious? Was he actually telling the truth? But if he was, why wouldn't he—

Callum finished the question for her. "Good grief, man. You need to talk to your wife. Why on earth wouldn't you have cleared something like that up, if you're actually telling the truth?"

Yes, why? Why, why, why? Noelle's brain screamed.

She didn't get to find out though. There was a huge woof, almost a howl, and a mighty crash in the underbrush. Sam and Jo's two dogs, followed by what Noelle could only think of as a monster—some hulking coffee-and-cream colored thing that must've weighed close to two hundred pounds—charged onto the path in front of her.

"Looks like we have company," Callum said, then hollered, "Go home, go home!" The dogs raced away, twigs breaking and leaves rustling in their wake.

Noelle knew she had no choice but to reveal herself. It would seem like she'd come from the main house just now, accompanied by the dogs. Good cover. She didn't know if she'd be able to speak, though. Her mind was flooded with conflicting, tormented emotions.

Either Cade was lying, though why would he lie when he was the one who'd brought up the topic? Why just not say anything? Or Cade was telling the truth. And there was only one reason for a man to let his wife think he'd slept with another woman when he hadn't. He was done. Didn't love her anymore. Didn't desire her. Wanted out of the marriage and knew it was the best way to make the break. And here all this time, well, until very, very recently that is, she'd been hoping, agonizing, trying to see if she could forgive him, if they could mend things . . . and all this time he'd been letting her think he'd been unfaithful because he didn't want to be with her anymore and didn't know how to say so. No wonder he'd been so calm before they left for Greenridge, when she said she wanted a separation. And no wonder he was being so "considerate" during this trip. Maybe she was wrong thinking he'd provide for her and the kids. Maybe he was trying to lull her into a false sense of security, so he could screw her out of support money.

There was only one thing she knew for sure: she wasn't going to tip her hand. Cade had cheated on her and this attempt to get Callum to believe he hadn't was just part of some strategy he was cooking up—or he hadn't but wanted her to think he had for the reasons her freshly stomped heart suspected. Either way, she wouldn't fall for whatever his plan was. She'd keep her mouth shut and watch and wait for him to reveal whatever clues he planned to and be grateful she had an inside scoop that things weren't necessarily as she'd first thought.

"Hey," she croaked, stepping out from around the side of the old cabin, lunch tray in hand. "Anybody hungry?"

Chapter 8

CADE FELT LIKE HE'D BEEN punched in the stomach twice. First when Noelle's voice came around the corner before she did. What was she doing there? What had she heard? Second when she appeared, all curvy and cute, her peaches and cream skin prettily flushed. She rested a huge platter of food on the edge of the unfinished deck.

"From Jo," she said.

"She spoils me," Callum said happily and yet again Cade was sincerely tempted to hit his brother. Smug bastard. No, not smug, he self-corrected, feeling even worse. Happy.

Noelle didn't look at Cade, just poured iced tea into two glasses and held out sandwiches for them to grab. A boulder of stress filled Cade's stomach and killed his appetite. She didn't seem curious or angry or relieved . . . or much of anything really. So maybe she hadn't heard the tail end of his and Callum's conversation? He didn't know if that was a relief or not.

As Noelle turned and put the sandwich plate down again, Callum caught Cade's eye, lifting his eyebrow in a silent, prodding question. For the life of him, Cade couldn't figure out what the goof was trying to say.

Callum sighed and shook his head. "Thanks for bringing us lunch, Noelle. You're spoiling us too." He grabbed another sandwich.

Oh, Cade thought. Of course. I'm an idiot.

"There's a ton of food," Callum continued "Do you want to eat with us? Cade was just saying—"

Cade choked on the mouthful of egg salad he was attempting to swallow. He waved his hands, trying to prevent whatever totally-bad-idea thing Callum was about to say, but he shouldn't have worried.

Noelle was already shaking her head and backing away, smoothly and politely excusing herself—escaping more like it.

Cade tried to keep up with Callum eating-wise after she disappeared, but every bite was like sawdust. Talking to Callum had been a disaster. Now his brother would push and push about why he hadn't told Noelle the whole truth, nothing but the truth. It was the shitty part of having a bunch of lawyers in the family. They grilled you about everything.

He was beyond relieved when two young guys Callum had hired to help with the roof showed up. For the rest of today, at least, he'd be able to avoid the inquisition.

Callum and the guys polished off the dessert, while Callum brought them up to speed about what he wanted done, but Cade only half listened. He knew, of course, that Callum was right. That he should come clean to Noelle. They should talk. Really talk. He just didn't know how. The words were in his head, but they never came out right and she always misinterpreted him. All he could hope was that if he stayed the course, loved the girls, provided for them and Noelle, and tried to be the guy Noelle had miraculously fallen in love with back in the day, maybe she'd see whatever qualities she'd first loved in him and love him again.

Chapter 9

IT WAS HARD FOR NOELLE to believe a full week had passed at River's Sigh and almost harder to believe that it had taken her mother-in-law, Caren, that long to get in touch with them. She'd known their schedule well in advance, plus both Noelle and Cade had left multiple messages.

And when Caren finally did call to arrange a visit with the girls, she didn't offer an explanation or apology for taking so long to respond, and she didn't mention a word about Duncan Archer, the girls' grandfather, her husband, either.

Now Eva and Emily were busy inside Chinook cabin, filling backpacks for a day out with "Nan," and Noelle and Cade stood on the porch talking with Caren. Personally, Noelle thought "Nan" was too warm a moniker for Cade's mother. It wasn't that Caren was awful. She wasn't. She was just too ... absent or distant or something to feel very connected to.

Meanwhile, adding to Noelle's discomfort, Cade stood so close she could feel the heat of him, and she was all too aware of their mutual tension. His was evident in every tight muscle and transparent comment. He practically folded himself in half trying to please the tiny woman who had somehow given birth to three massive men, telling her she looked great, asking her how her painting was going, how her gardens were doing, what her book club was reading. . . .

Noelle's own stress, though she had no idea if it showed in her body language or not, was mostly due to Cade's proximity and how hard it had been the past few days to stand by her vow and not tip her hand about overhearing him. She wondered what lofty, always-on-a-pedestal Caren would make of her son's behavior and when they separated, what Cade would say to his parents about the reasons.

In deep contrast to her and Cade, Caren was her usual soft-spoken, serene to the point of detached, self. She answered Cade's questions with just enough details to not appear rude, and asked him about how his work was going in return. Cade's face lit up, though Noelle could tell he was shooting for a nonchalant air, and he launched into a long description of a new project he was working on, a low-income housing complex.

His desperation to impress Caren, to be noticed, to perhaps get a tiny word of affirmation, twisted Noelle's stomach, but she found herself listening with interest. It had been a long time since he'd elaborated on any of his work to her, and this new focus was a world away from his usual contracts to build ever fancier, ever more expensive, sprawling homes in the suburbs for status seeking urbanites.

"Well, nobody can say you haven't found a practical use for an art degree," was all Caren said, as if Cade didn't also have a Masters of Architecture. Then she added, "Do you still paint, even a little?"

Noelle wanted to scream at her. At the very, very least, couldn't Caren, for once, just say Good job, Cade? And then she wanted to scream at herself for still caring about how Cade's crazy family cut him down constantly. It wasn't really her problem anymore, even if it did make her furiously sad.

Cade idolized his mom in a way that still managed to break Noelle's heart and fill her with impotent fury. His love for Caren was in every word he spoke—and every word he refused to hear against her. She, at best, seemed to remember he was her offspring.

"You just don't understand what her life was like," Cade used to say in the early years of their marriage when Noelle was young and naïve and thought everything and anything could be talked through and resolved.

"So make me understand."

He never could though. Or never would.

Conversation had solidly moved back to painting: Cade, unsurprisingly, saying that he still wasn't, but he still wanted to—and Caren, a tad surprisingly, encouraging him to take it up again, even just for fun.

Noelle moved to the cabin door and hollered for the girls to hurry up. She'd had almost all she could take of Caren and it was only their first visit.

Eva and Emily finally piled out the door with a clatter of noise and laughter—and enough stuff packed for a week away not just a day. They gave her and Cade long hugs, again like they were expecting a much longer separation, then headed for Caren's silver BMW.

Noelle waved as she watched the girls disappear around a bend in the long driveway, a veil of gray dust creeping behind Caren's car.

Cade stared after the vehicle, and Noelle wished it had occurred to Caren to ask her son if he wanted to spend the day with her, too. Out of an old reflex, she rested a hand on Cade's tensed forearm. He glanced down at her fingers, then at her face.

"So that's it, hey? They're off?" he asked after a beat of silence.

She nodded, moved her hand, and pressed her back against the cabin door. A long, shuddering sigh escaped before she could stop it.

"What's that about? Are you okay?"

Cade seemed genuinely concerned, and Noelle had a moment of weakness and said what was on her mind, mortifying as it was. "I was just thinking how, once upon a time, you and I would've jumped up and down with excitement at the prospect of a kid-free day all to ourselves."

"Oh, yeah?" Cade's eyebrow rose, but his tone wasn't belligerent, and he didn't appear to take her observation as criticism the way he usually did these days. "And just what would we have done in all that alone time?"

His voice was teasing and suggestive, and Noelle's heart clenched. How could you miss something as silly as a specific tone of voice so much? She almost wanted to flirt back, but she was so, so rusty. And really, honestly, was it even appropriate?

Disappointment clouded Cade's eyes for the briefest of seconds then was gone, but she'd seen it.

It was on the tip of her tongue to say, "Oh, we'd have thought of something." Not exactly a Rom-Com worthy line perhaps, but not the worst either—except Callum chose to appear out of nowhere. Cade turned his back to her at the sound of his brother's heavy work boots on the gravel, and her moment of silliness was gone. Which was for the best, right?

"I know I said we wouldn't work today, but we're making such good progress, I don't want to stop," Callum said. "And I cleared it with Jo. She doesn't need me. What about you? You got plans or are you in?"

Cade turned back to Noelle, a question squinting his blue eyes.

But she didn't know what he was asking, so she shrugged. "Do whatever you want."

He hesitated, so she helped him out. "If you want to work with Callum, work. The kids are away. I'll go see if I can help Jo out around the yard or something."

"Great. See you in a bit." Callum trotted off.

Cade didn't take a step.

"What?" Noelle finally asked after an awkward pause.

"I just, well, I don't know. Did you want to, uh, hang out together for the day?"

Noelle was so surprised that she laughed. It was a strangled, mirthless sound. "You're serious? In reality, what would we do together?"

She knew her voice, unlike his, held no trace of flirtation.

His jaw hardened, and he ducked his chin in a nod. "Okay, right. So I'll see you later then."

Noelle watched his broad shoulders and tight, rigid posture as he strode off and shoved hard against the regret coursing through her. So what if he seemed interested? He was only acting that way because she was the only option available to him right now. She wasn't going to be one of those sad saps that has sex with their soon-to-be ex then is all shocked when they still end up splitting. No, good-bye sex was not in the final pages of their story. Definitely not. She didn't need the humiliation of revealing herself to him that way anymore—and it would make parting with him that much harder down the road.

With the knowledge that she should be grateful

Cade didn't normally want to spend time with her heavy as lead in her heart—she was still too susceptible to him—she went off to see if Jo needed anything. Lunch was hours away, so it wasn't like she'd get stuck on Callum and Cade lunch duty again. Besides, wandering the bed-and-breakfast's pretty grounds the past few days had given her tons of ideas, and she wanted to see what Jo thought of them. She ended up getting an answer to that more quickly—and with more desperation on Jo's part—than she'd ever expected.

She heard the commotion before she saw the damage.

"No, no, no!" Jo yelled. "Bad dog. *Bad dog!*"

Noelle froze and craned her head—but still couldn't see anything. What could Hoover have possibly done? He seemed too enamored with Jo to ever do anything to displease her. Or maybe it was that other dog, the shepherd that belonged to Jo's sister, Sam (or, as Noelle still thought of her, the model-perfect blonde who'd eyed Cade and whispered secrets on their arrival night). She didn't even know if the mutt had a name. It seemed like everyone just called it Dog.

"Get out of here. Go, go, go!" Jo was out of sight and still yelling up a storm. Noelle walked faster, and Sam stuck her head out of the cabin she shared with her husband Charlie (a.k.a. the handsome writer guy; Noelle may not let herself visit much with everyone, but she had been taking an interest, trying to learn who they all were at least).

"What's going on?" Sam asked.

Noelle looked at her helplessly and shrugged. "No idea. She just started yelling."

The skinny German shepherd appeared from behind Sam's legs, so "bad dog" wasn't Sam's then.

There was a strangled, enraged sob—just one—then a loud gulp. "I can't believe it. I just can't believe it! Of all the stupid, rotten, miserable . . . " Jo's voice trailed off, and there was audible crying and a loud swishing sound—followed by a whooping bark.

Sam joined Noelle on the path and they both broke into a run just as a massive dog galloped through a cedar shrub. It flattened a group of lilies on the other side of the bush, then stopped, bizarrely, to nip the head off a bright yellow dandelion. The dog shook his broad-as-a-barn head in cheerful joy and raced away again.

Noelle recognized the beast immediately. It was the one that cut her spying on Cade short the other day, but Sam stared goggle-eyed. "What on earth?"

Jo tore into view, chasing along the trail of destruction the big dog had traveled.

The dog was long gone though, and Jo stopped dead when she saw her audience. Her face was red and blotchy, and her curly hair was a mess. Her shoulders sagged in such exaggerated unhappiness that Noelle would've laughed, except she knew Jo's upset wasn't feigned.

"Come. Look. See," Jo croaked in a dry-throated whisper.

Noelle and Sam, equally mute, followed Jo to the front side of the main house that provided visitors their first glimpse of the buildings after the long, scenic drive in. At first it was hard for Noelle to understand what she was looking at. The weather had been brutally dry for weeks. Where had all the mud come from? And why on earth was it dotted with blotches of bright pink, purple, and red? *Oh no.* Her brain caught up abruptly. She shot a glance at Jo who only nodded miserably.

"Oh, my . . . how, why?" Sam whispered. "Did that dog do all this?"

Another teary-eyed nod from Jo.

Every single flowerbed that Jo had slaved over that spring and summer, reclaiming from past gardens or building afresh, had been destroyed. The clearing that had been, until just recently, an overgrown eyesore—as Noelle knew from breakfast conversations—but that had been meticulously groomed into a beautiful green space, intended as the dinner spot for the reunion's anniversary dinner and dance, was hit as well. It honestly looked like bombs had gone off. Big holes and mounds of earth and clumps of destroyed sod marred the newly planted lawn. The biggest heartbreak was the flowers, though. Destroyed perennials and uprooted annuals lay in ruins everywhere, already wilting though the worst heat of the day was yet to come.

"It's our watering day. I thought I'd give everything a good soak," Jo stuttered.

Noelle noticed, then, a couple of sad overturned and trampled sprinklers still valiantly trying to do their job. One was sitting at a tipsy angle, spraying the house's lower windows. Muddy water tracked down the glass like silt-laced tears.

"I turned the hoses on and went to tackle the books, then that damned dog . . . he just . . . I didn't even know . . ."

"Well, alert the presses. There's a dog on this planet that Jo Kendall-Archer doesn't just love to pieces." Sam's misplaced attempt at humor fell flat; Jo didn't even react and Noelle could only stupidly flail her hands about.

"We have guests arriving tomorrow and the next day," Jo added. "We're booked solid right up until Callum and Cade's family arrives—and Duncan just called to ask if he could book a cabin for someone else yet again, so Callum's going to try to get that one he's working on ready. I can't . . . I don't have time for this."

Jo pressed her hands against her face as if she might weep again, but even if she did indulge in another cry, Noelle knew she was just venting. Any minute Jo would rally and suck it up and get busy— and Noelle was going to help her do just that. How could she not? The woman had to host the whole

Archer family and all their awful friends. The mere idea of it made her shudder.

She didn't think twice. She stuck out her hand and cleared her throat. Sam's eyebrows rose. Jo lifted her face and looked equally curious.

"Hi," Noelle said. "I know I've been introduced as Cade's wife, but I was wondering if you'd met me as your new landscaper? I was already intending to ask if I could tackle a few of your flowerbeds—admittedly not for quite this reason, but whatever. I work cheap—as in free. You just need to point me to the gardening shed and tools and tell me what your budget for the repairs is."

Jo stared. Sam clapped Noelle's shoulder and grinned. "Well, I have to say, Noelle, I always appreciate hired-for-free help. It's very nice to meet you."

Jo still didn't respond.

"Well?" Noelle tried not to be offended as Jo gave her a full up and down glance and didn't shake her proffered hand.

"Um, I don't know. It's a nice gesture, thank you, but you don't, you can't. . . ."

"I do. And I can."

"You aren't a gardener. I mean, look at you."

Noelle was mortified. Maybe this had been a bad idea. But she'd already stepped out on a limb. She forced courage she didn't feel into her voice. "I'm a bit soft, sure. Plump even. But I'm more than up for the work, I promise."

Jo's brow scrunched. "Plump?" Comprehension then horror replaced her confused expression. "I don't think you're *plump*. I think you're overdressed and pampered looking, like you haven't done a day's hard labor in your life."

Sam winced. "Really, Jo? Is it stick your foot in your mouth day and nobody told me?"

Jo had the good grace to flush, but Noelle grinned, bizarrely at ease. "Don't be silly. A person can change their clothing, Jo."

"See, Jo. It's not just me!" Sam quirked an eyebrow and nodded conspiratorially at Noelle. "I keep trying to explain how clothing works to her, but as you can probably tell . . . she doesn't get it."

At that dig, a tentative smile finally lifted Jo's downturned mouth and relaxed her tension-filled jaw. "What are you saying? That my holey tank top isn't high fashion?" Jo shook her head. "I'm sorry, Noelle. What I said sounded awful. I just meant . . . I don't know. I thought you came to relax and have a holiday, not to work your butt off."

Noelle shrugged and waggled her outstretched hand.

Jo considered her once more, then reached out and clasped Noelle's hand in hers, giving it a firm shake. "You're really sure?"

"Oh, I'm sure."

"Well, then can I ask you one more thing?"

"Of course."

"Can you be in charge of this one too?" Jo motioned at Sam. "She's almost as annoying as Cujo."

"That dog's name is Cujo?"

"No idea," Jo said. "But the shoe fits, doesn't it?"

"And now she tries to fit in and finally talks about shoes—way too late as always," Sam quipped.

"You guys are such brats! You remind me of my sister Melissa in the worst way." Noelle had been laughing, but now she clapped a hand over her mouth, shocked by the words she'd spoken. They were too casual. Too off the cuff. Her chest hurt and her heart pounded.

But if Sam and Jo noticed anything strange in her response, they didn't show it—just laughed too. "Well, I hope we're like her in some of the okay ways, too," Jo said.

Noelle's sinuses filled and the back of her throat ached. It had been so long, too long, since she'd enjoyed sibling silliness or the camaraderie of close female friends—a fact that almost-but-not-quite distracted her from what Jo had said. She had called her "overdressed and pampered looking"—so apparently Noelle had succeeded at one thing, though it only made her fail at a bigger thing. She fit in better with half of the Archer family, just not the half that she was starting to know and like. *It doesn't matter anyway, dummy. They're not your real family, and they won't even be your sisters-in-law for long.* The snarky thought—and the blow-to-the-gut reminders of Melissa—quashed the lightness bubbling through Noelle.

"Well," she said, hearing her own voice stiffen. "I guess I should get to it."

"Wait! Would you like to have coffee or something first?"

She really would. Deeply. And that was a big problem.

"No, that's all right. Thanks though. Cade's working. The girls are gone. I'd like to get as much accomplished as I can."

"Oh, okay . . ." Jo led Noelle to a small vine covered shed and pointed out various tools. Then, to Noelle's shock, she dug out a set of keys and a gold card and handed them to her. "For whatever you need to buy—and the truck so you can get back and forth."

Noelle nodded and after a few more minutes of assuring Jo that she had a plan, didn't feel "deserted" and that yes, she really was fine with it, she was alone with a shed full of tools and a pair of heavy gardening gloves.

She spent the rest of the day tidying and making mental lists of what she needed to buy to fill bare spots and cover holes once she knew what could and couldn't be salvaged. Destroy-a-con (as she, in her head, now called the T-Rex of a dog) had shown up twice, but seemed to comprehend that he'd crossed some line with the female humans on the property because he raced away the second his big brown eyes spotted Noelle.

"A rope," she muttered on his second appearance. "With one of those tether things you screw into the ground. That's first on the shopping list." It was probably her imagination, but she thought he galloped even faster.

She stopped only once, grabbing cheese and an apple for lunch, and a big water bottle to keep her company for the rest of the afternoon.

She was sweating like crazy—or crazier than usual, she should say—and her stupid control camisole and "super slimming" panties were wearing holes in her flesh, but still, all in all, she felt better than she had in days. The lawn was going to look fine with another watering or two; she'd managed to tamp down the sod in a surprisingly effective manner. You could hardly see where it had been disturbed. The plants and flowers that had been ripped out and thrown helter-skelter about the place were neatly lined up against their perspective beds, damp newspaper protecting their roots until she could get them back into the dirt.

She stood and stretched. Yes, there was no doubt about it. The weeks ahead of her were finally looking up.

Or so she thought until Caren appeared on the lawn, Cade in tow—and Duncan along for good (bad!) measure.

They all stared at her for a good ten seconds, and she could only imagine how she looked through their eyes: each of them fresh as a daisy, like they'd just showered and changed into clean clothes. She, on the other hand, was damp and sticky. In fact, she thought she could vaguely smell herself, a depressing, slightly gross notion. She probably looked like something Destroy-a-con had dragged in.

She'd totally lost track of time, darn it anyway, but seriously, it couldn't really be suppertime, could it? And Caren had planned to keep the girls until late. . . .

"Mom and Dad thought we could all go out for dinner," Cade said.

"If that's all right with you, of course," Caren added, scanning Noelle from head to toe. "The girls are washing up now."

Noelle had to physically refrain from hunching her shoulders and hanging her head under her mother-in-law's scrutiny. Duncan's once over was even less subtle.

"Well, at least some of the weight you put on went to your chest," he said cheerfully. "Some women just get fat asses."

Noelle's mouth fell open. Literally.

"Oh my God, Duncan. Really?" Caren snapped. It was something Noelle had never seen her do before: lose patience with her husband in front of other people.

"Dad," Cade growled.

"What?" he said obtusely, like the jackass he was. "It was a compliment. What woman doesn't want to hear she has a nice rack?"

Caren closed her eyes, her normally pale skin whiter than ever. She had tiny freckles—something else Noelle had never noticed about her. Did Caren usually cover them with makeup? Did she actually have a physical attribute she was self conscious about?

"I'm not really ready. I wasn't expecting . . . I thought you were keeping the kids until bedtime."

Caren's voice was resigned. "I'm sorry. That was the plan, yes."

"But plans change," Duncan interrupted. "And there's a swanky new joint I'd like to take you to. My treat."

"You don't need to treat," Cade said.

Duncan waved him off, stepped away from the group, and stared this way and that, suddenly red-faced and scowling.

"What the hell?" he huffed. "That woman of Callum's said she'd have the place spruced up in time. What the heck has she been doing? We can't have people here. It looks like a dump. I told them they bit off more than they could chew. Archers work with their heads, I always say, not their hands."

As usual, Noelle took issue with every word out of his mouth. It was obvious to anyone with half a brain that something had happened to the gardens, that this wasn't their usual state. And his stupid "work with their heads" line. Don't even get her started! Absolutely every time he could make a dig at his only son who had never practiced law, he did. Had he been a bear when Callum quit the firm too, or was it okay for

Callum to say no, just never Cade?

Sam appeared around the corner of the house. "Why, Duncan, such a pleasure as always." If she was being sarcastic, Noelle couldn't hear a note of it in her smooth voice. "Jo will be so pleased to hear your insightful, helpful comments about her workload."

Okay, correction. There was some scorn there, all right.

"Samantha," Duncan said. "Slumming again so soon?"

"That you call River's Sigh 'slumming' says way more about you than it does about the place, and, just to remind you in case you're getting a little soft in the noggin"—Sam tapped her head to drive the point home—"you're the one who booked your reunion here. Feel free to find another venue."

Duncan actually seemed speechless.

Sam continued, overtly chilly now. "Jo saw you drive up and asked me to double check with you that your 'final' list is actually final now. She was really polite as usual, but I have to say you need to stop being such a douche and stop dropping surprises on 'that woman.'"

A muscle jumped in Duncan's jaw.

Caren looked distracted.

Cade shifted his weight. "So what about dinner?" he whispered in Noelle's ear, making her jump and pulling her away from the flint sparking between Sam and Duncan.

"Why don't you and the girls go? You'll have a better time without me."

Cade cleared his throat. "Please?" he asked.

It hurt to swallow. It was hard to say no. But she did swallow. And she shook her head. For better or worse, Cade needed to figure out his own way to deal with his parents. She wasn't going to be the buffer anymore.

Chapter 10

EVA AND EMILY SKIPPED INTO view decked out in their best dresses, which Noelle had packed for just this kind of event. She smiled with relief. She and Cade might be failing on all kinds of fronts, but the kids they'd raised were lovely. Even Cade's parents had to see that.

"We're going to a super fancy restaurant. It doesn't even like kids to come, but they know Grandpa, so we're allowed," Emily said.

"I'm not a kid anyway," Eva interrupted, frowning. "And I'd be just as happy to go to McDonald's."

Contrary to her usual goal of always, constantly, creating a good impression and showing that she and her offspring were good enough for the Archers, Noelle found herself hoping Eva had said that very thing to her grandparents. Why couldn't Cade's parents be the kind of grandparents who took the kids out for burgers or bought fast-food for a sandy meal at the beach? Why couldn't they just want to get to know the girls, not feel compelled to use them to portray some stately patriarchal fantasy Duncan carried around?

"You'll have a lovely time," is what Noelle actually said.

Eva's eyes narrowed. "You're not coming with us?"

Emily stopped prancing. "Is it because you look like a total ragamuffin?"

Noelle glanced at Cade. He met her gaze and his eyes crinkled. He'd said the phrase so many times over the years, she could practically hear his voice now: "Kids say the damnedest things."

She grinned back before she could stop herself.

"Yeah, that's it, sweetie," she said to Emily. "That's it exactly."

Her heart hurt a little. Just one more thing she'd taken for granted and now she'd lose—shared moments of silent love, laughter or pain over something the kids said or did.

"You should see the waitresses. Doug hand picks them," Duncan said to Cade in a low voice. Caren ignored him. Cade winced. Noelle prayed the kids hadn't overheard and decided not having grandparents in their lives on a regular basis wasn't a loss. And any second thoughts she'd had about not accompanying them for dinner went out the window.

Maybe if she was someone like Sam, at ease and skilled at putting people like Duncan in their place, she'd have reconsidered. Duncan not only took whatever Sam dished out, he didn't attack her as mercilessly as he seemed to everyone else. Probably because she was in his class. Just as gorgeous. Just as rich. Just as strong personality wise, though not a dirt bag. But Noelle wasn't like Sam at all. And she couldn't bear watching Duncan run roughshod over his wife—the woman he was supposed to be honoring with this stupid family reunion and anniversary party—and his eldest son who he simultaneously bragged about being a chip off the old block (Heaven forbid!) and cut down and hurt every chance he got.

Maybe Cade's thoughts had turned along a similar path because his expression sobered. He looked at her again, almost beseechingly. "Please?" he repeated.

"I'll be fine, happy as a clam to have some alone time. You guys go," she reiterated, as if that's what he'd been asking, then whispered, "Hang in there. It's just three more weeks."

She'd meant her comment to be encouraging, but she could tell he'd taken it the exact opposite. He thought she was counting down to being free of him instead of marking days until they were *all* free of his family again for a few years. And who knew? Maybe she was.

Noelle waved and turned back toward the cabin, unable—*unwilling*—to watch Cade and the girls depart in the minivan, trailing after Cade's parents. It was too symbolic or something.

Chapter 11

THE AIR POURING THROUGH THE window was sweet and seductively cool. Noelle sought the digital clock in the dim light. 5:00 a.m. So there was a time in the day that wasn't brutally hot. Too bad it was unbearably early. Still . . . maybe she should get up now. The kids would be in bed for a few more hours. It would be lovely, for her and the plants, to get them into the dirt before the earth was scorching hot.

She rolled over, faking deep sleep, and patted at the mattress, trying to see if Cade had come to bed after he got home from dinner with his parents. If he had, he was already up. Callum was some crazy slave driver. She sighed, then jolted as she heard a purring sound from the corner of the room. She'd recognize it anywhere: Cade's ridiculously cute snore. She studied the shadows, found the big easy chair, and made out his long outstretched legs—still clad in the chinos he'd worn the night before.

So that's why he never disturbed her getting up at the God awful early times he disappeared in the morning. And why she never sensed his presence while she slumbered. He was sleeping in a flipping chair all night, after working hard all day. Maniac. She shook her head, half touched, half furious, and half heartbroken that he'd so wholeheartedly embraced her no physical contact rule. Half, half, half? Okay, so her math didn't add up, but that's how she felt: like every formula she used to count on was flawed and she always had the wrong answers or asked the wrong questions now.

Great. 5:02 a.m. and she was already morose. She made a decision. She would get up. She would get started. She was excited about her chores, yes, but also, anything was better than moping around, unable to get back to sleep.

She crept off the bed, selected clothing as quietly as she could, and grabbed her Spanx. She paused, studying the hated undergarment and reliving the previous day's temperatures and how awful it felt to bend, twist and dig wearing control top anything. It made something that should feel good and natural into torture. She threw the underwear back on top of her dresser. Then retrieved them again—and stuffed them into a drawer. Cade might not ever look at her or desire her again, but he also didn't have to witness her awful undergarments. She had her pride. Whoopie.

She had one pair of jean shorts, packed at Cade's insistence, in case they went out on a boat or fishing or something. (She could hardly imagine him doing either of those things, but he said he used to a lot.) She slid them on, sort of grateful to him. She only had dressy shirts though, or ones she wouldn't (shouldn't!) be caught dead in unless she was wearing a boob and belly wrangler. She hesitated, then dug through Cade's laundry on the floor and grabbed his white cotton button up shirt. He had a bazillion dress shirts. He wouldn't miss one. She slipped into a baby pink T-shirt bra—oh, the delightful softness of non-military strength support—and pulled his shirt on. It smelled like Cade, an intoxicating blend of figs and lime and his natural musk. When she realized she was taking a deep breath, reveling in the scent, she almost tore it off her back.

Stop being a moron, she commanded herself. It's just a shirt. It'll smell like you soon enough. She rolled up the sleeves that hung well past her wrists, then knotted the hem just below her hip. A square of folded paper in the shirt's breast pocket caught her attention. She withdrew it and slid it into Cade's empty suitcase. Then she pulled her hair into a ponytail, spared herself the mirror, and moved toward the door.

As she did, she passed Cade, still sprawled in deep sleep. She took in his frown and the crease between his eyebrows and wondered what sad, worrying things he was dreaming about.

Then she shook her head. She was up anyway. And this was stupid. His poor body bent in a chair all night. Beyond stupid.

She tiptoed over to him and leaned close.

"Cade," she whispered. "Cade. Come to bed."

His head turned toward her and his face relaxed, but he was still out of it. Must not have heard her. She gently rubbed his jaw. He leaned into her palm, but still didn't wake.

She shook his shoulder lightly at first, then a bit more roughly.

He shuddered awake. "What?" he croaked, his voice rusty. "What is it?"

"Come on. Come to bed."

Cade didn't make a move to leave the chair, just looked up at her from under heavy lids. "With you?" He sounded baffled, but grinned a little, his teeth a flash of white in the gloom.

"No, not with me. I just meant I'm up. You can stretch out."

A moment's hesitation. Then he let her heft him up and lead him to the bed, where he collapsed again, eyes immediately closed.

Noelle looked at him, coveting his maddening ability to sleep like a stone, wherever and no matter what was going on. His breathing slowed and he stretched out, wrapping his arms around her pillow.

Quietly, though she suspected a bomb could go off without waking him, Noelle stole from the room.

The sun had started its ascent, any moisture managing to coat the grass had evaporated, and Noelle was on her hands and knees, pressing earth around a beaten up azalea bush, when she heard a cabin door bang against a wall. The sound was surprisingly loud in the silence. She stood, walked a few paces, and saw Cade exit Chinook. He didn't notice her.

And then the quiet imploded. The girls spilled out the door after him, Jo let Hoover out pretty much the same instant, and Sam's cabin door opened and a tan and black streak zipped forward. There was a commotion of barking and giggling that turned to shrieks when Cade grabbed Emily and Eva, one by one, tickling them and holding them down, so the dogs had better access for cheek kissing.

"Blech, disgusting," he said cheerily. "The poor dogs have girl germs now."

Even Eva screamed with laughter and mock outrage. "More like disgusting *dad* germs."

Noelle watched them carry on like dog-obsessed lunatics all the way to the dining room. Just as Emily put her hand out to open the heavy door, Cade turned back. And spotted Noelle watching them.

His shoulders lifted in a question.

Ah, why not? Noelle thought. She was starving and lunch was a long way off. Besides not having to stop and make herself something would save her time.

She was a bit worried Cade might make breakfast into some strange confrontation or something, but he didn't. In fact, by the time she'd fixed a plate, poured a coffee, and found a seat by the girls, Cade was already dropping a kiss on Eva and Emily's foreheads and heading out.

"Aren't you going to eat?"

He didn't appear to hear; his step never faltered. Eva answered for him. "He always just has coffee and bacon. Then he gets off to work with Uncle Callum."

Ah, well that explained why he was looking so lean and mean these days. She considered her own bacon, two over easy eggs, and cinnamon bun, and grinned at Eva. "That's silly, hey? Who only has bacon when there's homemade baking around?"

"*Right*?" Eva said.

Emily giggled.

The girls were happy to spend the day playing with the dogs, cavorting in the yard and creek, and doing the odd chore for her or Jo. Noelle had thought they'd get bored, but they didn't. The furthest thing from it, actually.

It was like they thrived with the freedom to roam the slightly wild property and do their own thing—free to read and rest and work without a scheduled event, music lesson or sports practice. Not that those things were bad. Noelle stood by the fact that they helped kids develop abilities, hobbies and talents that would round them out as adults, enhance their personality and give them pleasure. But maybe in her attempts to give them every opportunity she'd forgotten that an important part of childhood was just being a kid. Goofing off, daydreaming and playing pretend were all things that developed an inner life and resiliency, perhaps better than any formal engagements, classrooms or workshops could.

And speaking of which. It was beyond interesting, maybe even a bit alarming, that she'd had more deep thoughts, more fun, more daydreams, more plain old comfortable, stress free moments the past two days, than she'd had in, well, an overly long time.

The girls were off cheerily helping Jo with something and the grumble in Noelle's stomach suggested it was nearing dinnertime, when Cade and Callum tramped across the lawn. She stood up awkwardly, overly conscious of how her dusty, perspiration-dampened shirt clung. Plus her bare legs, scraped by thorns and bug bitten because she'd forgotten to put on bug dope, were filthy—literally stained a brownish green from the dirt and grass she'd kneeled in all day.

Callum looked around and let out a low whistle. "Wow, you weren't kidding when you told Jo you'd get it fixed up. If I hadn't seen the worst of it yesterday, just after you started, I'd never believe it was destroyed."

Noelle's face, already warm with the afternoon heat, flamed with pleasure. "Thanks. There's still a load to do, of course, and lots of empty spots that really show since everything got disturbed, but I'll do a quick shop tomorrow and by tomorrow night it'll look better than ever—" She stuttered to stop. "I mean, not better, but just as good."

Callum grinned. "Well, we really, really appreciate it." He clapped Cade on the back, said he'd see him later, and headed off, leaving Noelle and Cade alone.

Cade was scrutinizing her, arms folded across his chest, eyes narrowed and glowing an impossible blue in his sun-darkened face.

"What?" Noelle hated the defensive note in her tone. She shifted her weight, resting one hand on her hip, rubbing the back of her neck with the other. "I know I'm filthy and sweaty. I'm working. Deal with it."

"That wasn't what I was thinking. Not even close."

Noelle shifted again, insecurity writhing through her. He was probably shocked by the weight she'd gained now that it was all loose and out there for him to see, but no way in hell was she going to tell him whatever difference he noticed was because she wasn't wearing support underwear.

All of a sudden Cade's expression morphed. "Wait a minute! That's *my* shirt."

His hand shot out and for half an instant Noelle that he was going to grab her breast. What the—

He didn't though. Well, that wasn't his focus anyway. His fingers patted the shirt's breast pocket, then tugged it open.

"Cade, what the hell?"

He was already stepping back. "Where is it?"

"Where's *what*?"

"You know."

"I have no idea—" She broke off. "Wait. Do you mean that piece of paper?"

Cade glowered. "Of course. You didn't wash the shirt with it inside the pocket, did you?"

"What? No. I put it in your suitcase."

"Did you read it?"

"What? *No*," Noelle said again, feeling like she was buffering, stuck on the same point, repeating and repeating. She hadn't even thought to read the note—something that now seemed like a big mistake. "What's the big deal anyway? What's in it?"

Cade didn't answer, just rushed away, no doubt to check her story and reclaim the mysterious paper of oh-so-utmost-importance.

Her stomach rolled with suspicion, and she had the ridiculous urge to sprint after him, beat him to the house, see what—or whom—he was hiding from her. But fat lot of good that would do. Even running full out, she couldn't catch him if he didn't want her to.

Sighing heavily, she kneeled and picked up her trowel once more. The earth was warm and comforting, honest and obvious, under her hands. She had her answer. The conversation she'd overheard between Callum and Cade was a ruse—for what point, she had no clue—but obviously Cade had cheated on her. Something in the paper probably proved it, though why she even needed more proof was a better question. She'd seen him and Sherry with her own eyes, so why had she latched onto his stupid lie to Callum in the first place? Because she was pathetic, that's why.

She tamped down the earth around a replanted geranium a little too firmly.

You could actually ask him straight out one more time. Talk to him. I know it's rocket science, but—she killed the nagging voice of so-called reason. There was no point asking a liar anything, once, twice or a million times. That was the whole point. They lied.

And even now she didn't know what hurt most—his infidelity or that he'd lied. They'd always said that was the one thing they'd never do. They'd never *lie.*

It was almost dark when she finally stood and surveyed the results of her day's labor. With the exception of a few bare spots in the flowerbeds, the yard, after just day two, looked pretty much blemish free. It was amazing how quickly well-established, deeply rooted plants could recover from trauma. The thought depressed her further. She used to believe, all starry-eyed and stupid, that the same was true for humans. Now she wondered if it was the reverse: damage the roots of a human relationship and the whole thing was irreversibly harmed, leaving you powerless while it withered and died.

Chapter 12

TWO AND A HALF WEEKS, two and a half weeks, two and a half weeks. The words, part encouragement to press on and part threat, ran nonstop through Noelle's head as she crossed the gravel path and cut across the lawn toward Jo and Callum's. Overhead the evening sky was a deepening shade of mauve, a sure sign that days were getting shorter and summer was nearing an end, regardless of how the soaring temperatures contradicted the fact. A few bright stars popped out here and there, and the evergreens sheltering the cabins around River's Sigh whispered in the merciful breeze that kicked up. A slightly fishy yet sweet and fresh scent of water and campfire smoke carried in the air from somewhere down river. The whole sensory experience should've been calming. It wasn't. It was the furthest thing from it, in fact.

Noelle's stomach was one big knot, a knot she was all the more conscious of, confined as it was, for the first time in days, back in her "tummy taming" under-wear. She tugged at the hem of her short A-line dress, hoping everyone else dressed up, too. She still couldn't believe Duncan was having a "stag" night—a big moron night was more like it. Cade and Callum had already left to meet Brian, a few of Duncan's old buddies, and the man of the evening himself. Noelle had done all she could to wiggle out of the girls' night, but Jo had been persuasive and Noelle, craving the company of female friends, had been weak, so there she was.

A new trio of thoughts replaced her two-and-a-half-more-weeks mantra. *Do not fall in love with this awful place. Do not fall in love with Jo and Sam's silliness. Do not make things harder for yourself.*

And then she was there, walking into the front entrance of Jo's home, not the big, shared dining hall for B & B guests at the back. A cloud of good smells—garlic and butter, spices and heady wine—enveloped her, and laughter and voices floated down the hallway.

"Noelle!" Jo exclaimed, like Noelle was a dear friend, not some stranger she'd met for the first time that month. "You made it."

"Good grief, Jo, it's what, a five minute walk? It's hardly a miracle she showed up." But Sam handed Noelle a chilled glass of something pink, like she too had been hovering by the door in anticipation of Noelle's arrival, no matter how she razzed her sister.

"I'm just really glad you came," Jo said. "And you look lovely."

"Me too," Sam said. "And you do."

"Thanks," Noelle said, ridiculously shy again as

her cheeks warmed.

"Come get settled, and let me introduce you to everyone—and promise to eat your face off. There's tons of food."

Before one of them could move, however, a siren-like lament started up outside. It sounded like the noise a whale crossed with a gorilla might make.

"What on earth?" Jo asked. Sam looked anxious, too.

Noelle laughed. "Don't worry. That's just Destroy-a-con."

"Destroy-a-con?" Jo asked, no less confused.

"Yeah, that big mutt. I don't know who the owner is, but if he thinks that dog can have a free reign of terror, he has another thing coming. I intercepted it earlier tonight—just as it was heading to the big side flowerbed—bribed it with food and hooked it to a tether I bought the other day."

Sam grinned. "I thought Dog was excited about something when I left tonight. She must've heard the big goof complaining about being tied up."

"That's actually your dog's, the German Shepherd's, name then—*Dog*?"

"Yep," Sam said. "Poetic, right?"

"Or practical anyway."

Sam chuckled at Noelle's words, but Jo shook her head. "I'm sorry, Noelle, but I really don't want to keep that dog."

"Keep it?" Noelle interrupted with horror. "Me neither. I want its deadbeat owner to track it down, preferably before it howls the night away. His home can't be too far off. It's always here. And, worst-case scenario, if no one claims it, I'll take it to the pound."

Jo gasped. "I don't know. That's pretty awful."

"It's not awful. It's smart," Sam corrected. "It looks like an expensive dog. Someone will come for it, and maybe the owner will learn a lesson. It's dangerous for a dog, especially a dog that big, to wander constantly. Someone will think it's a bear and shoot it."

"Or they'll know full well it's a dog, but it will act the way it always does and they'll shoot it just for that." Noelle and Sam laughed.

"I don't like it," Jo said.

Noelle glanced over her shoulder, checking for Caren. When she didn't see her and was confident from the volume of the chatting guests in the other room that no one else would overhear, she whispered, "Alternatively, we could present Destroy-a-con to Duncan and Caren as an anniversary present."

Sam hooted. "I like the way your mind works."

Jo looked horrified and Noelle had mercy on her. "I'm only teasing. I'd hesitate to give those two a plant, let alone a pet of any kind."

Jo laughed, but then softened the mockery. "Caren dotes on her dog, actually."

Noelle shrugged. "Yeah. If only she could pass some of that affection to her boys."

Sam's eyebrows rose. "Wow, and I thought *you* weren't fond of your in-laws, Jo."

"Speaking of which. Where is Caren anyway?" Noelle asked.

As if cued, the phone rang. Jo answered it, carrying the handset to another room. When she returned, her brow was furrowed. "Well, that's weird."

"What is?" Sam asked.

"That was Caren. Apparently something's come up. She won't be joining us."

Noelle grimaced. "I was just being a smartass. I don't really have a huge problem with Caren or anything. Is she all right?"

The crease in Jo's forehead deepened. "That's what I find so strange. When I asked her that very question, she laughed, sounding totally cheerful and relaxed, and said, 'I'm great, better than great actually, so don't worry about me. I just can't make myself come over.' Then she wished us all a good time, apologized for 'making me work for nothing,' and hung up."

"Was she drunk?" Sam asked.

"I don't think so, but on that note . . . maybe we should join the rest of the party before they send out a search crew."

When Noelle stepped into the living room on Sam and Jo's heels, they—plus the small crowd of five other women—burst into rowdy applause. Noelle startled.

Jo patted her arm. "Sorry, we weren't trying to

freak you out. It's just that I told them about the dog/flowerbed disaster and what a life saver you've been."

Noelle ducked her head. "Well, thanks. It was nothing. Really."

"No, it was definitely something—and something I would've had to tackle if you weren't here, so thank you," a curly-haired pixie of a woman said. The speaker's voice was familiar, and Noelle suddenly realized it was Aisha. With her hair down, wearing a pretty sundress instead of her usual ironic T-shirt and jeans, Noelle hadn't even recognized her at first.

"Well, you do always seem to have your hands full, so you're welcome." She looked around for Aisha's baby. "Childfree night?"

Aisha's nose wrinkled in a half smile, half wince. "It's Mo's first time with a babysitter that isn't Grandma or Gramps. I hope she'll be okay."

"She'll be great. She's a trouper," Sam said. "But if you want someone to go check on her, say the word."

Aisha shook her head, her smile broadening. "Sheesh, you guys are so obsessed."

"Guilty," Sam agreed.

It was hard for Noelle to get her head around the idea that Sam was a *grandparent*. What was she, late thirties, forty max? "You sure don't look like any grandmother I've ever seen," she said aloud.

"Well, good grief, I should hope not," Sam exclaimed. "And it better stay that way for another thirty years."

Laughter spread through the room, Jo made introductions, and Noelle tried to keep up. Herself, Sam, Jo, and Aisha—then four others: Diane and Terri, introduced as Caren's best friends, Beth, described as a mutual friend and the owner of Bookish, Greenridge's independent bookstore, and a lady named Tabitha. Noelle didn't catch her connection to Caren or Jo, but decided it didn't matter.

The appetizers kept coming in an amazing array and variety, everything from piping hot artichoke dip with tortilla chips to shrimp skewers and sushi rolls. Noelle cursed her underwear yet again, though they didn't keep her from having "just one more bite" of a dozen different things.

"I planned a few games," Jo said at one point, when their eating and small talk slowed. "And I'm more than willing to still play them, but without the lady of honor . . ."

The room quickly and unanimously decided that shower games to celebrate the thirty-fifth anniversary of someone who wasn't even there were unnecessary. And almost as quickly, as if they'd wanted to make sure they stayed long enough to be polite, but were watching for an exit, Diane, Terri, and Tabitha said their good-byes. Beth, begging an early morning, followed shortly after.

Noelle almost sighed with relief as the group shrank and became more familiar. It wasn't that she hated crowds exactly, she just wasn't immediately and easily at home with everybody and anyone like Jo seemed to be. And she definitely wasn't the life of the party like Sam—though she wondered if some of Sam's vivacity, at least in part, was something she worked at because as soon as the other women left, Sam relaxed and became less overtly "on."

Then another thought occurred to Noelle and she was surprised by how disappointed it made her. "Well, I guess I should head out too, hey? Let you guys enjoy sister, mom and daughter time?"

Sam, Jo, and Aisha stared like she'd spoken gibberish.

"No, please don't leave me alone with Miss Practical and Ms-Even-More-Practical," Sam implored. "I love them, but I see them all the time. I need to visit someone who wears heels—hell, shoes, even."

Noelle laughed. Both Jo and Aisha were indeed barefoot, and both she and Sam wore pumps. Her own were strappy sandals, worn in the hopes of looking a little taller and a little thinner, a sedate two inches high. Sam's, on the other hand, were cream-colored stilettos that looked like extensions of her long sleek legs.

Noelle felt a little like Miss Piggy by comparison, but decided to keep that unfortunate observation to herself.

"Yes, please stay," Jo said. "I'll feel totally ripped off if you leave now, just when the real festivities can begin."

"You *have* to stay," Aisha announced melodramatically. "It's my first night out as a mom. I can't go home before ten o'clock, even if I would love nothing more than to crawl into bed and sleep like the dead right now. How lame is that?"

"Not so lame—just sounds like motherhood to me," Noelle said.

Aisha's eyes creased at the corners in response to her words, and Noelle remembered how isolated parenting babies could be, how you never knew if what you were feeling was normal or not . . . and she'd had a husband to share everything with. She lifted her wine glass to Aisha. "Don't worry. In another eight years or so, you'll get to sleep regularly again."

"Thanks *a lot*," Aisha said, but her creases deepened.

Noelle's raised beverage caught Sam's attention and it was topped up before Noelle could blink.

"And now you have to stay," Sam said triumphantly. "You have another glass of pink lovely to finish."

"Twist my arm, why don't you?"

Sam grinned. "I have to say, you look like you wanted to be convinced."

"Well, how can I say no when you're all so desperate for my company?"

Aisha giggled, Jo laughed, and Sam's grin broadened.

"But seriously, I really did want to stay, so thank

you." Then, maybe because the wine in her system was making her sentimental and lowering her inhibitions, or possibly because she couldn't deny it anymore or didn't want to, she added a rush of words that shocked her. "Thanks so much for including me and for being so nice. Since my sister died I feel like I have no one to talk to about bad things, no one to just be stupid with, no one to, well, ah . . . " Her voice trailed off. "Just no one, I guess."

Silence, complete and heavy, met her words. Noelle's gut churned and she knew her face was probably a brighter pink than her drink. What had she gone and done? Why had she killed their lighthearted fun when they were just getting to know each other?

"Your sister *died*?" Sam asked with no trace of her usual dry humor or droll indifference. She sounded about eight—and like she might burst into tears. "That's terrible."

"Yeah," Noelle said, her throat hot and full. Sam's simple words held a bizarre amount of comfort. Her sister had died. And it was terrible. "Almost two years ago now, but I only miss her more and more, never less." And then, since she'd wrecked the party anyway, knowing from there on out they'd give her a polite greeting, then run as fast as they could whenever they saw her coming, she said the other thing she needed to get off her chest, needed to tell somebody, even these kind virtual strangers, just to have it out of her, to ease the weight that was crushing her while nobody even knew anything was wrong.

"And my marriage is over. This whole visit is a farce. Some big last hurrah that Cade wanted to take as a family." Noelle's hands were shaking, so she set her glass down on the nearby coffee table, constructed from a large, gleaming tree burl. Its solid, practical beauty only emphasized how weak and pathetic she felt. "As soon as we get home, we're separating. We're calling it a trial but I know once I leave, it will be permanent."

More silence. Noelle hunched forward and pressed her hands against her face. They hated her. And why shouldn't they? What was she thinking putting this on them? Of course they weren't saying anything. What, after all, was there to say?

Chapter 13

THERE WAS A SOFT CLINK as someone set a glass down next to hers, then a hand pressed against her shoulder. Here it comes, Noelle thought. The comment about how it had been fun, but wow, look at the time. And she'd agree, apologize and leave.

"I'm so sorry." Jo's voice was empathetic, but calm and completely irritation-free. "Callum had mentioned your sister, but you seemed so composed, like you were doing fine. I didn't want to be intrusive by offering condolences when you obviously didn't want to talk about her. I'm sorry if that was cowardly of me."

"If I'd known what you're going through, I totally would've fixed up the gardens and yard, not let you deal with them alone. I had no idea. . . . " Aisha said.

"No." Noelle lifted her face and looked first at Jo, then at Aisha. "I wasn't saying any of this to get sympathy or make you feel bad. You didn't need to say anything, Jo. There is nothing to say—and the garden work is sanity saver, I promise." She laughed a little raggedly. "And just think. This is me sane. Imagine what I'd have been like without the yard work. Maybe I should thank Destroy-a-con."

Jo patted her shoulder once more and sat back on the couch.

Aisha shrugged. "Sometimes you just have to keep putting one foot in front of the other, and hope that things get easier, that you understand more some-day. . . ."

It was such a curiously old-souled thing to say, both wise and sad, that Noelle forgot how self-conscious she felt and found herself wondering about Aisha's story instead. How had she come to be a mom so young? How was it to meet up with your biological mother, and then have her and your adopted father fall in love and get married? What were the things she was struggling to understand more about? Before Noelle could figure what she should say, if anything, Sam spoke—to Jo.

"I told you they were on the rocks."

"Seriously, Sam?" Jo practically hissed.

"Yes. Remember I whispered to you that first night—"

"I meant *seriously, you're bringing that up now*? Shut up."

Aisha widened her eyes and gave an exaggerated I-never-understand-them shrug. Noelle felt herself grin and she gave Aisha a return shrug. And interestingly, she wasn't mortified or humiliated to have it confirmed that Sam had been talking, maybe even gossiping, about her. She was only curious.

"So that's what you were whispering about. How could you tell?" Noelle picked up her glass again and sneaked another bacon-wrapped date, while she waited for an answer. Now that the worst of her inner mess was out on the table, so to speak, she was fully at ease with Jo and Sam for the first time since they'd met. She really liked them, and had felt bad being a big phony around them. She was a wreck and now they knew it. And she wouldn't be in their lives for long, and they knew that too. There was something freeing in all that knowing, in not having to pretend anymore.

Jo glanced at her. "You aren't bothered?"

"Not at all. Besides I'm the one who brought it up. All's fair and all that."

"Your body language," Sam said smoothly. "I was pretty sure of it that first night, but watching you guys the past weeks confirmed it. No matter how close you stand to him, you're always separate, carefully poised and saying and doing the right thing—but alone."

"Well, not just me. Him too, right?" Noelle asked, wanting to make sure that Sam wasn't putting the breakdown of their marriage solely on her shoulders, that she was using "you" in its plural sense.

"Nope. Just you. It's fascinating, actually. He works a group and socializes like a pro, but has eyes only for you. All his focus is on you. You seem focused on him, but all your awareness is on everyone else."

"Well, I'm so pleased we're such 'fascinating' entertainment." Noelle's throat was suddenly dry, and it was hard to swallow the last bite of bacon and date.

"I'm not saying it's your fault, just that I think you're the one calling the shots."

Noelle choked on her wine. "What? No. That's ridiculous. Nothing could be further from the truth."

Sam shrugged. "Maybe he did something you can't forgive, fine. But if you want him back, you can have him back—in a heartbeat. If you don't want him, you probably have good reason, so own it and act on it. But don't whine and waffle around. If you're serious about leaving him, you shouldn't have even come on this stupid trip."

"He's her *husband*, Sam." Aisha's voice carried the outrage Noelle felt, and she was grateful because she couldn't have squeezed out a word if she was paid to. "The father of her *children*. It totally makes sense if it's hard for her, no matter what he's done. She probably agreed to come to see if they could work things out. That's what most people would do."

Noelle opened her mouth, figuring she might be able to respond now. She didn't get an opportunity.

"It doesn't make sense," Sam argued. "If you're miserable with someone, no matter how good your relationship used to be, if you know it's done, why waste your time? Everyone in this room has already learned the hard way: Life's short—sometimes too short."

Aisha turned an angry mottled red and looked ready to blow a gasket. Jo held up a hand to stave off her bellow and turned to Sam. "Fair enough. Life is short, yes. But let's stop talking about hypothetical situations or in general. Think about Charlie."

Both Aisha and Sam went rigid at the mention of his name, and Noelle realized with some guilt that *she* felt fascinated by the dynamics unfolding in front of her. Maybe Sam hadn't meant anything offensive by her earlier comment.

Jo continued, "Right now you're still in the crazy-good honeymoon phase of love."

Sam's mouth curled: part smile, part defensive snarl. She ran a finger around the rim of her glass. "And your point?"

"My point is, imagine out a few years. Life happens—as it does—some good, some bad, and you guys aren't communicating as well or as much as usual. Maybe his career tanks. Maybe one of you gets sick or depressed. Anyway, for whatever reasons you don't feel the love. In fact, maybe worse, you don't even feel the *like*. What do you do? You just bail, of course, because life is short and heaven forbid you 'whine' or 'waffle around' regarding something like ending your marriage."

"Dammit." Sam's fair skin paled to marble. "Of course not. *Of course not.* It goes without saying that we had better never fall out of love—but we would not just end it. We would fix it. And if we couldn't fix it. *I* would fix it. Or . . . " Her eyes, already such a vivid green, went a shiny, glimmering jade. "Ah, shit. Shit! I'm sorry, Noelle. I'm a little new to this whole true love shtick. I forget how it complicates everything. It's very annoying."

Aisha crossed her arms over her chest, but she seemed more relaxed than she had a moment ago. She gave a small half smile, shaking her head a little.

And as for her? Well, Noelle almost had to laugh because really, what else could she do? Sam was . . . unique.

Noelle's wine glass was magic—or Jo was— because the thing never emptied. She sipped it gratefully, happy to hide behind it.

Jo made another round with a fresh bottle. Aisha and Noelle accepted a top up, but Sam declined, holding her hand over her glass. She directed her piercing gaze at Noelle once more. "Did you guys used to have a love worth fighting for?"

Noelle shrugged. "I thought so."

"Not good enough. Did you or didn't you?"

"Good grief, Sam. This isn't an inquisition."

"It's fine, Jo. You don't need to protect me from Sam."

Sam shot Jo a victorious look.

"And as for your question . . . once I would've said yes. A hundred percent yes, but now, well, I just don't know. I'm not sure he loves me anymore, and I'm pretty sure he's been unfaithful. There's no way back to what we used to have—or not that I can see anyway. And I'll be damned if I end up like Caren, you know?"

Jo and Aisha nodded solemnly. Sam shook her head, but appeared thoughtful not disagreeable. "Are you sure?"

"Sure that I don't want to end up like Caren?"

"No, sure that he cheated."

"Of course, I'm sure. Why would I make something like that up?" Noelle recalled the conversation she'd overheard between Cade and Callum though, and her stomach tightened.

"I'm not saying you made it up. I'm just asking if you're sure. He doesn't seem like the type."

"Why on earth would she say it if she didn't know it?" Jo asked. "And you just met Cade. How would you know what type he is? Callum says that of all three boys, Cade is most like Duncan."

A familiar wave of indignant fury sloshed through Noelle, despite the topic being Cade's possible infidelity. Surprisingly, it was Sam who defended him. "That's a load of bullocks. I'm sure he's not a cheater, but even if he is, you can talk to Cade for five minutes and know he's no Duncan Archer."

Again, Noelle was more curious than offended by the implication that Sam didn't believe her about her own husband's unfaithfulness. She didn't have to ask for an explanation though. Sam turned toward her. "He's friendly and social, but he doesn't flirt. He hardly even seems to register female attractiveness. I have no doubt that his aloofness is a magnet and women throw themselves at him all day long, wanting the ego boost and validation that his attention would provide—men too—but he's immune. I'd actually put money on it. If anything he's more like Caren, bottling everything up."

"That's . . . very interesting," Noelle said. And it was. How many times had she thought that very thing, even just that week? Come to think of it, even Caren and Cade's unvoiced yearnings were similar—except instead of hoping for the affection from a spouse that would never be forthcoming, in some ways Cade was forever a sad little boy craving parental affirmation. She sipped her drink, mulling that over.

"Holy cow," Aisha suddenly announced. "It's after midnight. I actually do have to go or I'll turn into a pumpkin."

And she was right. A huge clock that looked like a set of rustic gears said it was ten after twelve. Where had the time gone? Noelle didn't feel done talking, not by a long shot—but they all had a lot of work to do the next day.

Jo looked equally reluctant as she got to her feet.

Noelle winced, feeling shy again for the first time in hours. "I'm sorry I was such a downer. Not much of a festive girls' night."

"Are you kidding? It was great. I'm sad you're going through such a hard time, but we felt an affinity for you right off the bat, didn't we, Sam?"

Sam rolled her eyes, but then nodded and her smile was soft. "Yeah. I have no idea why, but you already seemed like someone we knew—or wanted to."

Noelle—and it was definitely not because of the wine now—wanted to weep a little. "Well, thank you. That means more than I can say."

"I kind of want to thank you or something too," Aisha said. "Sometimes I think everyone's life is working out easily but mine. It's actually comforting to know that someone as put together as you, with kids who have turned out as nice as yours, also has shit hitting the fan."

"What does that mean?" Sam frowned and touched Aisha's arm. "Have you heard something else from Evan that you haven't told us?"

Aisha laughed shakily. "Not since his last stupid surprise visit and out of the blue going-to-go-for-custody threat, no . . . unless you count the letter from his creepy lawyer that arrived yesterday."

"And you waited until now to tell us about it?" Both Sam and Jo practically sparked with outrage.

"I wanted to spare myself your freak out until I've spoken to my lawyer, a.k.a. Callum, but now's not the time. It can wait until after the big reunion."

"Are you sure?" Noelle asked, knowing it wasn't her business, but feeling completely stressed anyway. She'd totally hijacked the evening with her issues when Aisha was facing some custody battle or something.

"I'm totally sure, and it was nice to get to know you better," Aisha reassured her, then held up her hand to ward off another outburst from Sam. "I'm serious, Sam. We will talk about it and deal with it, but a few days won't hurt. I checked."

"Okay . . . "

Aisha nodded. "Good. It's settled then."

Noelle thought she looked pensive though, despite her bravado, and couldn't help but notice she was chewing the corner of her lip. Then she twitched her shoulders abruptly, like she was shrugging free of an itchy blanket or something, and grinned. "Let's not make this painful, guys. It was a great night—though I admit, next time we should definitely shoot for more laughs-a-minute and less sad goat."

Noelle patted Aisha's shoulder and followed her lead, lightening the mood. "Agreed, but hey, wait a minute. Who's the sad goat in this scenario? Me? Thanks a lot."

It was a good note to leave the house on and shared laughter buoyed her across the lawn. She'd only gone a few steps, however, when she turned back.

"Hey, Sam," she called.

"Yeah?"

"What's that pink wine called? It was delicious and I might need more of it sometime."

"Therapy," Sam yelled back.

"Ha ha, I know. But what's its name?"

"*Therapy*. I'm serious. Pink Freud by Therapy."

Noelle laughed so hard she almost peed—and Jo, Sam and Aisha giggled, too.

"So tonight was what? *Group* therapy?"

There was more laughter as she raised an arm in one last farewell, though she had no idea if they could see her silhouette or not. Jo's heavy wooden door clunked shut, and gravel crunched as Sam and Aisha went their own ways, taking the divergent paths to their cabins.

Noelle stood a moment longer, breathing in the warm stillness and watching the moon. It was huge and yellow and hung lower in the sky than usual. It filled her with a strange yearning that she didn't quite understand—maybe that life could be this beautiful and tranquil all the time.

She paused again when she arrived at the stairs leading up to Chinook cabin's porch. Though she knew her family slept within its walls, no one was waiting up or had thought to leave a light on for her. Its windows were dark and showed no signs of life. The bubbly effects of her therapy waned. She just felt drunk.

Chapter 14

ALL THE LIGHTS WERE OFF in the cabin, but the moon was shining brightly through the big windows and Cade's eyes had adjusted to the shadows. It occurred to him that it might be difficult for Noelle to see when she returned, however, so he padded barefoot down the stairs, thinking he'd turn one light on at least. The kids had been tough to get to sleep, hyped on sugar and excitement. Despite their energy, or perhaps because of it, they were exhausted though, and now, finally, were totally conked out. A parade wouldn't wake them, let alone him moving through the house.

The front door clicked open and he froze on the stairs. He was too late. Noelle was home. A soft clunk on the hardwood floors told him she'd kicked off a high-heeled shoe. Then there was a shuffle and thump. Had she lost her balance standing one footed? The second shoe dropped. She made a shhh sound, as if telling herself to be quiet, which struck Cade as hilarious. She was obviously tipsy. He wasn't sure what to do—as usual. Continue down the stairs and ask how her night was? They couldn't avoid each other forever, could they? Or respect her obvious desire to do just that and sneak back upstairs and pretend to be asleep?

The closet in the kitchen that housed a washing machine and dryer opened, and a motion sensor bulb sprang to life, throwing a rectangle of light through the doorway.

Oh, what the hell. He might as well let her know he was back, too.

He stepped into the kitchen—and stopped, swallowing hard.

Noelle had her back to him and she'd just unzipped her dress. As he watched, it slid down her body in soft pink-orange blur and puddled at her feet. In the weird, super modest underwear she'd taken to wearing lately, she was extra beautiful—like one of those 30s movie stars or something, her waist accented by the confining fabric, her curvy butt refusing to be fully contained and peeking out the bottom of the elasticized briefs.

She stepped out of her dress, still facing away, opened the top of the washing machine and leaned forward. He inhaled sharply.

"Ah, hey . . . Noelle?" he whispered.

She jumped and shrieked like he'd screamed at the top of his lungs, then turned toward him, hand on her creamy chest. Her breasts were held high in their satin constraints—so beautiful.

"Er, I was just going to put on a load of towels," she said.

He didn't bother to pretend he wasn't gawking. "And you're doing that in your underwear because . . . ?"

Her ivory cheeks flushed. He'd always liked her coloring. She was like a peach or something and could never hide her feelings, or didn't use to be able to anyway. Nowadays—he cut off that line of thought. She was actually talking to him. He didn't want to wreck it.

"I . . . uh, don't know. Maybe I was getting ready for bed but got distracted by the laundry." She motioned at a basket of striped beach towels. "Or maybe I was hot—"

"Yeah, I'd say you're hot all right. More like super hot."

Noelle's eyes narrowed and Cade flinched. Way to go, idiot, he thought. Ruin the conversation with a badly timed stupid comment. You guys can't just flirt anymore. You lost the right—but then, miracle of miracles, Noelle bit her lip and smiled a little. Cade's blood surged.

"Oh yeah, super hot. That's me all right." She motioned down at her body. "Especially in this getup."

She sounded so like her pre-their-marital-disaster self that Cade almost laughed with happiness, but he didn't want to risk the moment, risk her taking it the wrong way. He cocked an eyebrow instead and gave her an appraising look—and was further encouraged when she returned it in kind, scanning his T-shirt and boxer clad body. What was this? Was he going to get lucky with his wife? He was infinitely glad he'd showered the bar smell off himself when he'd gotten back from driving his dad home.

"Would you like a drink?" he asked.

"Mmm, I've had a few already," she admitted.

"Just a few, huh?"

Her eyes crinkled at his teasing. "Okay, twist my arm. Sure."

He poured her glass of sparkling rose before she could change her mind.

"Are you trying to get me drunk, sir?" She stepped toward him, loose limbed and a tad unsteady on her feet.

"I think you managed that yourself."

"What else do you think I can manage myself?" She waggled her eyebrows and Cade, normally not a huge fan of alcohol, saw its perks.

"Want to sit in the living room?" she asked.

Did he? Hell, yes. He hesitated, then grabbed another glass and the open bottle and followed her into the living room. She held her arms out and pirouetted slowly in an exaggerated manner. "It's a nice place, isn't it?"

"It is," he said, nodding—then poured himself a glass of wine and downed it like a shooter.

She settled into the sofa, took a long sip of wine, and looked up at him.

He grew uncomfortable under her study. "What?"

She averted her eyes. Shrugged a little. "Do you think you'll ever kiss me again?"

Cade's core tightened. "I don't think. I know."

"Oh, yeah?"

"Yeah. If you want me to that is."

There was a long pause—and then she nodded just once.

Cade took her glass and she let him. He set it on the coffee table beside his own and sank to his knees on the floor in front of her. She shifted, opening her legs to him, and he moved forward, closing the space between himself and the couch—and the distance between them—with his body. Her thighs rested alongside his hips. Her chest pressed against his. He responded to the sensation of her soft flesh and heat instantly. Neither of them verbally acknowledged the erection tenting his boxers, but the flirtatious quirk of one eyebrow and the way she bit her bottom lip said she'd noticed. Then she looked down and stroked him with her gaze. It was as effective as a hand job and he stifled a groan. If there was one advantage to being cut off for so long, maybe it was this. His pecker was a monster.

Her smile broadened and her eyes glinted. "So is that a gun in your underwear, or—"

He'd even missed her corny jokes, but it wasn't the time to indulge them. He wanted to indulge something else. "Funny." He gripped her hips, pulled her even closer, and lowered his mouth to hers. He lightly nipped her bottom lip—then almost lost it when she shuddered against him, apparently as immediately turned on as he was. Her pubic bone pressed hard against his hardness, but the promise of softness, so much softness, was so close. She opened her mouth to him and he found her tongue with his, flirting with it first, then kissing her deeper, more intensely. She tasted boozy and sweet, and he was lost in the scent of her, the feel of her. How had they ever fallen away from this when they were so damn good at it?

Then Noelle's fingers were wrapped in his hair, and she was leading the kiss, bending over him, angling his face upward, gently flicking his tongue with her own—then biting him just sharply enough that he felt it but soft enough that it never became pain, only triggered a slow burn of pleasure and promise.

"Cade," she moaned and grinded her pelvis against him in a slow undulating circle. "I want you in me. Now—"

He extricated himself from her grip. "Not yet."

"Please," she said, throatily. "Please. Don't make me beg."

"Maybe I like it when you beg."

She pushed against him so forcefully and felt so warm and wet that he almost forgot his intentions to prolong the encounter as long as possible. He closed his eyes against the desire rocking through him and fought for control.

He slipped a finger under the edge of her panties.

The things were like a chastity belt—but they were damp and lovely with her wanting him and damn if that didn't give them their own sort of weird appeal. He rubbed along the heat of her and she made a noise that was practically a purr. He leaned sideways, reaching for the nearby lamp.

She tensed.

"What's wrong?" he asked.

"No lights."

"Since when?" He tugged the lamp's chain. A soft glow filled the room. She averted her eyes and turned her head from him, but he gently touched her chin and made her face him again. "Yes, lights. I love watching you."

And he probably needed the light to get her out of the contraptions she was wearing.

She squirmed uncomfortably and seemed on the verge of tears. He winced.

"Okay," he whispered. "Okay."

He stretched up and over, clicked the light back off, and kissed along her jaw, her neck, and finally her clavicle as he lowered himself to the floor once more. Resting a hand on each of her thighs, he studied her in the shadows, shadows made all the deeper for having had and having lost the light in such quick succession.

Outside the window, the moon moved across the sky and halted, big and full, so low to the earth it seemed to rest on the nearby mountains. Despite her wishes for darkness to hide in, Noelle was fully illuminated, silver and beautiful, but instead of being further aroused, something quaked inside Cade at her expression—so solemn, so removed, so distant from what it had been seconds earlier.

He bent his head and kissed the soft skin between the high waistband of her underwear and the low band of her bra top. He was overcome suddenly with everything he wanted in that moment and rested his head on her knee. She smoothed her hands over his scalp, stroked his hair . . . but instead of comfort, he felt terror.

He scooped his hands under her ass and pulled her off the couch, onto his lap. Then in one fluid motion, supporting her weight in his arms, he spread her beneath him.

On her back now, bent legs cradling him, she arched her spine, lifted her hips and shimmied out of her tight undergarments. He reached around her and undid the clasps on her bra. And suddenly there she was, laid out in all her glory beneath him, naked in the moonlight. She was so lush and full he could hardly breath. Here and there, where the elastic of her under-things had bit into her flesh, little red pressure lines marred her creamy skin. He kissed away one of the fading marks. Why did she do this to herself? Why was she always trying to rein in, control, punish the curves he loved?

"You're so beautiful," he whispered.

"*Please,*" she breathed, wrapping her hands around

his head and tugging his face toward her chest.

His cock throbbed as his mouth closed around one of her nipples and a sharp keening sound escaped her. His fingers grazed her other nipple, gave a little tug, then moved lower—much lower. When he found the molten core of her, she buried her face in his neck and writhed against him, trying to stifle the noises she could no longer keep from making.

"Mmm, so you like that, hey?" He knew the words would drive her crazy, and he hoped talking would slow himself down. It wasn't working.

"So much," she groaned. "So much—but hurry." Her voice was more air than sound. "It's been too long. Hurry."

Cade sank himself into Noelle. She exhaled with something like relief and bucked against him, pushing for a faster finish even while she whimpered in pleasure at the deep slowness of his movements. "Is this what you want?"

"Yes," she moaned. "*Yes*."

He lost the ability to speak. I love you, he thought. Then she too could only groan as he rocked her, rocked them—willing her to feel him, to know him, to want him. Her body tensed then trembled, and she buried her face in his shoulder, trying to quell the sounds she was making. He couldn't hold back any longer either. He exploded in physical release and pleasure, but with something bigger too: profound relief and joy. They were fixed. They were good. They were back together the way they always should be.

"Noelle." He breathed her name, part sigh of pure, almost painful ecstasy, part prayer of gratitude.

"Cade," Noelle whispered back, sounding equally undone.

He eased out of her, pressed his lips to her soft stomach, then stretched out beside her, propping his head on his folded elbow and taking her all in.

He wished she wouldn't, but he didn't resist or say anything when she immediately reached behind her, felt around on the couch, then pulled a knit blanket down and covered herself. He didn't want even that much of a barrier between them.

She pressed her palm to his chest over his heart. Could she hear it still hammering away, pounding out a rhythm that said how much he loved her? He hoped so.

Cade wondered if he'd ever felt so good. The old saying was right. You don't know what you've got until it's gone—or in his case, until it's almost gone. Well, actually he'd always known what he had. What they had. And he was beyond relieved that Noelle had realized it too.

The effects of contentment and good sex worked their magic and he dozed off. He had no idea how long he'd been asleep for, but the room was a light gray-blue, like dawn was struggling to arrive, when Noelle's voice stirred him.

"What are we going to do, Cade?"

He rolled closer and tucked an arm around her. "Well, a little more of this and that, I hope, and then, I don't know, take the kids to do something fun or—"

"That's not what I meant. Not with the kids tomorrow or in the immediate future. I mean about us. Long term. This"—she made a large sweeping motion with her hand as if to encompass a whole lot of who knew what—"it's no good. It's too confusing. Too painful. We have to stop."

"*What*?" He wheezed like he'd been punched hard in the gut. He'd heard all her words, but he couldn't make sense of them. "What do you mean stop? We just fixed everything. We're good again, aren't we?"

Noelle raised her eyebrows and in her face, just inches from his, he saw something terrible. Pity. Sympathy.

"We had sex, Cade. *Drunk sex*. You don't honestly think that changes or fixes anything, do you?"

Cade lumbered to his feet. He hadn't been drunk. He'd had one beer and a gulp of wine the whole night. But he felt completely bombed now. Shell-shocked. Leveled.

His throat raged with fire and his eyes had a strange itchy feeling. He wanted to say something, anything, starting with, I . . . I don't understand. Please explain where you're coming from because I'm totally lost . . . but the words that ripped from his gut when he finally managed to swallow the lump blocking his speech came out as a yell. "What the fuck, Noelle?

What. The. Fuck?"

"Shhhh, you'll wake the kids."

Cade shook his head furiously. Whatever she was starting now and her biggest concern was that they'd wake the kids?

She had risen to her feet now too, bringing the blanket with her. She tightened it around herself. Yeah, heaven forbid he see her naked or something.

Cade pressed his fists into his eyes. Felt wetness. And fury. "What was this? That?" He motioned back and forth between them, unable to form more words.

Noelle reached as if to put a hand on his shoulder, then pulled back. "I'm sorry. I was tipsy. And horny. And God knows I want you. I always want you. It's not enough though."

The words crushed Cade. "So you just wanted to have sex with me—or someone anyway. You don't want me. You don't want us."

"It's not that simple."

"Yes, it is. For me. It is."

Noelle had soft black smudges under her eyes from her makeup, but her look was hard. "Well, that's just great, Cade. Perfect, in fact. I'm glad everything's so simple and clear for one of us, at least. But if that's true, why'd you screw around on me—on our family? Why will you never have an honest conversation about what happened? How can you act like you want me, only me, then hurt me so badly I want to ... " Her voice trailed off and her whole face tightened. "Never mind."

"So badly that you what?" Cade felt like he was bleeding.

Noelle shook her head. "You act like you're the injured party. Like I'm the one being cruel. So I wanted a piece of ass tonight—and I chose yours. Sue me. Maybe if you'd done similarly, we wouldn't be in this mess."

Cade threw up his hands. "I've told you a hundred times—"

"Don't yell at me! And yeah, I know what you told me. And I know what you told Callum. And I know what you really want, a good little wife sitting at home because it's convenient and whoever else on the side whenever the urge hits. After all these years I've finally figured it out. You are like your dad—but you know what? I am not like your mother. I'm not going to fade away to some pathetic, gray version of myself just because you can't—or don't want to—keep your dick in your pants."

Cade's whole body sagged. It was too much effort to stand and he sank onto the couch. Even Noelle thought he was like his dad. Even Noelle. . . .

He covered his face with his hands, but she didn't relent. Didn't let up.

"If you don't like what I'm saying, explain how I have it wrong. Show me what I missed. Give me anything that proves what I say isn't true."

"I told you it was nothing. We didn't really do anything." His voice was angry, dammit, when all he felt was sorrow. Why couldn't she get it?

"It was something to me, Cade. Really something—and that's why *we* have nothing." Noelle's voice dried up and splintered away. She swallowed hard, found it again. "Don't ever tell me it's simple. Don't you dare."

They stared at each other, and for Cade it was almost like looking into the face of a stranger. She hated him. They were both shaking—Noelle so hard her teeth banged against each other. Cade knew what this had cost her. She dreaded confrontation as much as he did. They were both way more comfortable with cold silences—though look where those had brought them. He wanted to reach out, to try to comfort her, but they were way past that now.

Tears streamed down her face as she stooped to retrieve the underwear they'd torn off in their earlier frenzy.

Go to her, you friggen putz, a voice in his head yelled as she left the room. Stop being such a pussy. Lay it all on the line. But Cade didn't know how. He'd just look like a fool, she'd still think he was lying, and it wouldn't help.

Chapter 15

NOELLE PRESSED HER BACK AGAINST the wall in the master bedroom and tried to stop crying. If she didn't get a grip, she'd have a full on sob fest. She couldn't push Cade's face out of her mind—how he'd crumpled when she said he was like his father. But she also couldn't bear how she'd let him in, had shown him again, no question, how much power he still held over her heart and body.

No matter how she'd enjoyed the moment, when she realized what he thought it meant—that they were fixed—she'd had to address the things that stood between them. Lashing out was the only way she could build a wall and protect herself. She was so damn weak when it came to him. Every bit of her wanted to fall for his sweet talk—and his even more persuasive body language.

She clutched her stomach, trying to soothe the sorrow and tension aching through it. She couldn't bear how genuine Cade's attention felt and how badly she wanted to believe it meant he wanted her, only her, the way she wanted him. Was that how he'd made what's-her-face feel too? Was there more than one what's-her-face? How would she even know, really? It was a fluke she'd found out about them in the first place.

She squeezed her eyes shut. She knew better now though, didn't she? He could lie. And it didn't matter how much it hurt, she meant it with every fiber of her being: she would not follow in Caren's footsteps.

His anguished eyes burned in her memory again. And she realized something she hadn't before. She had the power to hurt him too. If she needed anything to solidify and cement her decision for them to break up, this was it. They had to stop intentionally damaging each other—and unintentionally damaging their kids—before it was too late and they wouldn't even be able to be civil to each other for Eva and Emily's sakes.

She wrapped her arms tightly around herself, but felt no comfort. Funny how leaving him was all she'd thought of the past few months and now that the time was drawing close, she felt no relief, no justified outrage, only a deep throbbing awareness of every-thing she'd—they'd—had and lost. Okay, not funny. Awful. Beyond awful.

Chapter 16

CADE WAS HIGH UP ON the scaffolding, painting the soffit and fascia on the newly sided south-facing wall. He wanted it done before the temperatures were too blistering. When Callum arrived, he was almost half done. He glanced at his little brother. "Well, lookie, lookie. Decided to come to work, did you?"

Callum stretched his arms over his head and groaned. "You're insane. How can you not be hung over? The only reason I'm even here is that Jo begged. The reunion starts in three days, and she's desperate to put some old friend of Dad's here—some idiot who can't stoop to staying in a local hotel."

Cade climbed down. "I don't have a hangover because I'm smart enough not to get drunk with my old man."

"And here people say you're a dumbass."

"Yeah, well, they call you worse."

"And today they'd be right."

Cade grinned, but it faded as he surveyed their progress on the cabin. "It's starting to look good, but there's no way we'll have it ready in time. The exterior will get done for sure, so it'll be protected for winter, but the inside? For guests?" He shook his head.

Callum grimaced. "Yeah, I know. And initially the whole reunion deal was that the daily festivities and meals could be here, but overnight guests—with you and Noelle and Aunt Sharon's family being the exceptions—had to stay elsewhere. We're a small operation right now, as Dad knows full well. Minnow is Aisha's permanent rental. Sam and Charlie have Silver. You and the girls are in Chinook. That only leaves Rainbow for Auntie Sharon and Spring here, which, like you said, isn't going to be serviceable in time. And most people booked early, but leave it to Dad to have one friend who's too good for that, then expects the whole world to adjust on its axel to accommodate him."

"Any chance Sam and Charlie's new place will be ready?"

"In three days give or take?" Callum shook his head. "Not a chance. And it's not like they're sponging. They booked Silver in advance for four solid months. They won't even accept a discounted rate."

Cade tossed a dirty paint rag into a garbage can by the corner of the cabin. "So tell Dad to shove it."

"Yeah," Callum said. "The way you do, right? Like it's that easy."

Cade shrugged.

"But speaking of good old pops. What did you do to piss in his whiskey last night?"

"Are we working or talking?"

Callum sat down heavily on the flattened grass, pulled his shirt off, and stretched out. "Talking and having a fifteen minute siesta. We might as well since we're not going to finish this place in time anyway. Then we'll go make ourselves useful to Jo in some other way."

Cade stared at Callum. "I don't mind continuing to work on the place for the next few weeks, while you do something else."

"Nah," Callum said easily. "I've stolen enough of your time from your family as it is."

Cade sighed, pulled off his own shirt and dropped to his butt beside Callum. The early morning sun did feel good, especially compared to the killer heat that was sure to come later. It was also good to see his muscles looking like he used them again. He wondered if Noelle had noticed. She used to make comments about his body all the time, which was totally embar-rassing—but also kinda hot. He liked that she got turned on just by looking at him. Liked that they got turned on by looking at each other. Just another thing he missed.

"What did you do to your neck?"

"What do you mean?" Cade rubbed his throat, but didn't feel anything out of the ordinary.

Callum leaned in, squinting. "You've got a bruise or something. Maybe it's a bug bite? It almost looks like a hickey."

"What?" Cade asked.

Callum started to laugh, hard. "Oh my God—it *is* a hickey. You're eight shades of red. Did you get lucky last night when Noelle got home?"

"What are we? Fifteen? Fuck off."

"So you did. You totally did." Callum stretched again—then paused mid-stretch and narrowed his eyes at Cade. "Wait a minute. Tell me it was Noelle who gave you that. You were with your wife last night, not one of those sleazes Dad was hitting on."

Cade's stomach clenched and he felt sick. "Of course I was with Noelle," he seethed. "I told you, like I told her, I don't cheat on her."

"So . . . I'm confused. You're moodier than ever, but last night you guys were together, so shouldn't you be happy things are getting sorted out?"

Cade planted his fists hard in the ground beside him and launched himself to standing. "A guy would think that, right? Let's get back to work."

Callum shook his head and stayed exactly where he was. "You're an idiot."

Cade exhaled loudly, but didn't say a word. He just couldn't catch a break, could he? Not one, ever. How the hell had he not noticed he had a damn hickey of all things? And when, for that matter, had Noelle ever given him a hickey before?

"What? No comment? No denial?"

Cade just glowered.

Callum stared at him. "Tell me what happened. No holding back. Obviously there's a bunch I don't know.

Noelle used to be crazy about you—and you used to be crazy about her—but now you're letting her go without a fight?"

"What?" Cade felt sucker punched. It was actually difficult to pull air into his lungs. "How did you—"

"How'd I know this trip's one last family hurrah, before you and Noelle separate? Well, not from the brother I've been working and shooting the shit with all day and night, that's for sure. Noelle told Jo, Sam and Aisha last night. Jo told me—but don't worry. She won't tell anyone else."

Rage and sorrow fueled Cade with a pulsing energy and he began to pace. "She's telling people? She's actually telling people?"

"Cade." Callum's voice was softer now. "Come on, man. What the hell happened last night?"

Cade kicked the metal garbage can he'd just deposited his paint rag into and sent it careening away from the house. Garbage and bits of unsalvageable, useless remnants from their labor spilled everywhere.

"Calm down." Callum stood too. "I know you don't like to hear it—but you need to learn how to communicate. Considering how much whatever you said to Dad last night pissed him off, you obviously can get your point across when you need to. Use your words and pray it's not too late."

"I can't." Cade was still now, all energy spent. "I don't know what to say. I don't know how to put it."

"So you're just going to what? Keep avoiding her

every chance you get and hope she'll magically interpret your behavior as desperate love and devotion instead of avoidance and disdain? You think not looking her in the eye and being willing to suffer some embarrassment or shame will somehow convey the message that you didn't cheat?"

"You don't understand anything."

Callum shook his head in disgust. "That, big brother, might be the one thing you've got right. I don't understand. At all. How can you tell me you love her and want to make your marriage work, but not even speak to her? You can sleep with her but you can't talk to her? I don't get it. And I don't even know if I think you should get to have her if this is your idea of how she deserves to be treated." He scooped his shirt up.

Cade balled his hands into fists. All he wanted to do was punch something, someone. And Callum knew it.

"I thought you'd changed, that you seemed different this trip. I actually believed you when you said you wanted to make your marriage work and felt bad for you. . . ." Callum shook his head again. "But you haven't changed at all. If anything, it was your early years with Noelle that were different, an act to keep her maybe—but a leopard can't change its spots. And I guess you can't keep up the ruse anymore, or she sees through it. Sucks to be you."

Words again. So many of them. Callum may have quit practicing law, but he hadn't quit using words as his weapons. And his little brother hit his mark each time, drawing more blood, causing more pain than Cade's occasional punches ever had.

He felt himself staggering, like each comment was a physical blow. He had changed. He had. Or maybe he'd never even been what his family always thought he was in the first place. Noelle had never thought he was. But none of that mattered now, did it?

His arsenal was limited to physical things, an ability to work and provide, to put food on the table and a nice roof over their head, to touch and give pleasure . . . and Callum was right. Noelle deserved better than that. She deserved the kind of husband who could be everything she needed, the provider, the faithful lover, a trustworthy friend, the confidante she lacked now that her sister was gone. . . .

"Cade?"

Callum was saying his name. He hadn't left yet and Cade hadn't even noticed until now. He lifted his head just as Callum rested a hand on his shoulder. "I . . . I'm sorry. I shouldn't have said . . . any of that. I'm an asshole. I didn't mean it."

"It's okay," Cade said. His tongue felt thick and his body was slow, like his blood had thickened and his heart was having a hard time pumping oxygen through him.

He looked into Callum's blue eyes so like his own and as he had ever since they were kids, though he'd done a piss poor job of it every fucking time, he wanted to protect him, make him feel better. "Don't worry, little bro. You didn't say anything I don't already know."

The expression on Callum's face told Cade he'd failed once again. The words he'd meant as comfort had only made his brother feel worse. Seemed to be his thing. He squinted his eyes shut and spoke through gritted teeth. "Do you really think talking to Noelle could tell her anything that my actions can't show her?"

Callum stepped back, then nodded slowly. "I do. They say a picture or gesture is worth a thousand words, but I don't know. I think it's easy for actions and gestures to get misunderstood."

"But I'm not good at it . . . at sharing my feelings, I mean." Even now, even here, desperate, he could hardly spit it out.

"Who is? But at least if you try to explain it and she still leaves you, you'll know you really did all you could—not just that she failed some secret-known-only-to-Cade test. How can anyone know anything unless they're told?"

"I just . . . I just wanted her to know the man I am without having to tell her. She knows me. She should know how much I love her. I shouldn't have to explain it."

Callum's eyebrows shot toward his hairline again. "Dude . . . how on earth did you guys even make it this far?"

Cade shook his head. Hearing himself through his brother's ears, he realized he sounded like an idiot. "I don't know. It's a mystery."

"It really is," Callum said. "Seriously."

But Callum's words were the opposite of discouraging. Cade had left the cabin that morning thinking that was it. His marriage was over and there was nothing he could do. Now he realized it was just the next level of his test. And he would kick this level's ass. He would do whatever it took to fix their marriage before it really was too late—including trying to explain himself and his mistakes and his lame attempts to remedy things.

Chapter 17

NOELLE WOKE AND THE CABIN, as usual, was quiet. No doubt the girls were already out and about. And Cade? Well, he, no surprise there either, was long gone too. She kicked one of the couch cushions that he'd brought upstairs to create a makeshift bed out of the way. Prior to the girls' night, she'd thought she couldn't possibly see less of him than she already was. The past three days since they'd had sex—and she wanted to roll up into a little ball of regret and raging hormones whenever she thought about it—had shown her that no, she was completely wrong about that. He was like a ghost or something, an entity other people referred to occasionally and that moved the odd dish or towel, but that you never actually saw. And that was a good thing, right? Absolutely. Of course.

It occurred to her that she was protesting too much, even to herself. The idea made her frown.

She showered, did her face, then blow-dried and flat ironed her hair instead of just pulling it into the quick ponytail she'd come to appreciate for its simplicity, speed and coolness the past few days. Then she slowly—and a bit resentfully, if she was honest—got dressed in full support underwear, slacks and a silk blouse. She was going into town to do some shopping for Jo, then meeting Caren for lunch, sans Eva and Emily—a request from her mother-in-law that made her wonder what was going on.

Outside, Destroy-a-con leapt to his feet in delight at seeing her and bounded over, the light chain that bound him jingling on its tether. She noticed his food and water dishes had been filled and made a mental note to thank the girls later.

In a flash, she extended her arm and held her palm up. Just in time, too. Mid-jump, he sank back to his haunches.

"Down!" she said, even though it was kind of dumb because he already was. "Good dog." That last line was a stretch, but it made him wiggle with what she interpreted as happiness, so obviously he was starting to understand her. She gave his silky ears a rub.

She was not a dog person (understatement of the year!), but even to her, it was bizarre that no one had responded to any of the posters she and the girls had stapled to power poles along the highway or to the Facebook notice Jo had posted. Destroy-a-con looked expensive and well cared for. Clean, he was very handsome—if unbelievably huge. And Jo figured he was young, not much older than a year or so. Someone should be looking for him. Ah, well, two more days and Noelle would contact the pound. It didn't make her happy and she said a little prayer that the owner would make an appearance.

Destroy-a-con gave a soft whine and looked up at her expectantly, but continued to sit perfectly still. His fur was still soft and shining from the brushing she'd given him when she first put him on the lead. In an impulsive move she didn't quite understand she knelt beside the big oaf, wrapped her arms around him, and hugged. It was like snuggling a life-sized stuffed animal and oddly comforting. He wriggled with barely contained joy at the affection, and she stood just before he managed to lick her face.

Laughing, she glanced at her mini van—then at her phone. It wasn't even nine-thirty. How she wished she didn't have to go into town! All she wanted to do was work in the flowerbeds. Jo had given her full reign in the yard now, expressing surprise and then gratitude when Noelle asked if she could tackle the other over-grown beds and perennials along the various paths, too. But instead of getting to it, she was dressed up and looking forward to a lunch she'd enjoy about as much as a root canal at the dentist.

She sighed, darted another look at her phone, then kicked off her pumps—making sure they were out of Destroy-a-con's reach. Taking a minute to look at the roses wouldn't hurt. She trod shoeless across the short-clipped lawn. When she was a kid, she could practically sprint barefoot over broken glass, her feet were so calloused from running wild outdoors, spring through fall. Now she felt every little bristle of grass against her soft soles. It was wonderful.

Noelle had just stooped, hand cupped beneath a vibrant pink bloom, when someone cleared his or her throat behind her, making her jump.

She turned to see Sam, who was wearing a huge grin and shaking her head. "I can see I'm about to lose my only ally to the Jo side." She motioned at Noelle's bare toes.

Noelle laughed. "Yeah, I guess."

Sam studied her, and opened her mouth as if to speak, then shut it again.

"What? Out with it."

"Hmm, no, it's nothing."

"*What?*"

"Forget it. I don't have a lot of women friends. I don't want to wreck my chances with you by opening my fat trap."

"Well, at least one part of you is fat anyway. Makes me feel better."

"Har har," Sam said, her grin big again.

"Now, seriously, tell me."

Sam shook her head once more and alarm spiked through Noelle. She crossed her arms and settled her weight on one hip. What had she done to Sam that was such a big deal that Sam wouldn't even bring it up, lest it wreck their fledgling friendship?

"Tell me right now. You're freaking me out. Whatever I did to bug you, I'm sorry. I'm sure I didn't mean to. I'll fix it or whatever."

"Oh . . ." Sam actually looked a tad flustered. "It's nothing like that. Nothing you did."

"So tell me already!" Embarrassment flooded Noelle's cheeks and she knew she was beet red. Great.

"It's just . . . don't be mad. I don't mean it badly. I really don't."

Noelle widened her eyes and raised her hands, shaking them in a would-you-just-spill-it-already gesture.

"You're really pretty, but you dress like a seventy-year-old matron." Sam laced her fingers together, then extended her arms and cracked her knuckles.

Noelle blinked.

And yet another person snuck up on her from behind. Jo. Her slightly anguished "What the hell, Sam?" told Noelle she'd heard Sam's comment and was equally mortified by it.

Noelle looked down at her ensemble. It was expensive. And lovely. And yes, perhaps, a mature look—but good grief, she wasn't a kid anymore. She had kids.

"I hate not being taken seriously, especially by Caren and Duncan," she said. "And at least this outfit hides my pudge and camouflages my chest."

Sam snorted derisively.

Jo frowned. "You make a lot of fat jokes. You know you're not fat, right?"

Noelle raised her eyebrows and shook her head at Jo. "Sam? Comment on that, please."

Sam's eyes narrowed. "You're not thin, but you're not fat—and who cares if you were?"

"Easy for you to say."

"It's easy for anyone to say. If you want to lose weight, lose weight—but don't hold it against people who aren't heavy that you are."

"She's not heavy!"

"No," Sam agreed with her sister. "But she's not a stick."

"And that's why I wear modest, as you so kindly put it, seventy-year-old-matron clothes."

"Seventy was probably a slight exaggeration," Sam admitted. "But you're not doing your curves—or your desire to be taken seriously—any favors with the clothes you wear. And on that last note, you could put on a power suit, but if you don't take yourself seriously, expect and demand respect, you won't get it anyway. It's about attitude, not wardrobe."

"So I should just start sporting too small V-necks and mini skirts and bear all?"

"Yeah, *that's* what I was saying." Sam rolled her eyes and Noelle remembered that she was the one who'd asked Sam to tell her what she was thinking, had practically begged actually—and now she was doing exactly what Sam had worried she would: shooting the messenger.

"Okay, fine."

"I don't mean it as an insult. I just mean . . . you seem uncomfortable in what you're wearing, like it's a uniform or an expectation or something, not what you really like to wear or feel at home in. A lot of women rock a constant business casual look; it suits them, ha ha, pun intended."

Noelle groaned and smiled despite herself, but her agitation returned almost as quickly. "I'm not you. I can't wear stilettos and skinny jeans or pencil skirts all day."

"Who says you have to be me to look good? Look at Jo. She's not stick thin and she wears jeans and beaten up flannel and tank tops every chance she gets, but—"

"She always looks great," Noelle said archly.

"Yeah, uh, where are you going with this?" Jo asked, but she was smiling and obviously couldn't care less what Sam thought of her apparel. And she also wasn't wearing anything remotely like what Sam described. She was in leggings and a flowing tunic-styled shirt. With her curls pinned in a casual updo and semi-precious stones dangling from her ears, she looked every inch the carefree, comfortable-in-her-own-skin spirit that she was.

Looking at her, and getting to know Jo even the bit she had, Noelle totally saw why Callum had never gotten over his high school sweetheart, and though it seemed like the lovely nonsense of a romance novel or something, it was beyond cool that they'd somehow managed to reconcile whatever their huge hurts and issues from those earlier days were and ended up together fifteen years later. She needed to ask Jo the story sometime—

Shoot, Noelle thought. She was doing it again. Making plans for the future with these family members that weren't going to be part of her life much longer. She sighed heavily. She'd never learn.

Sam eyeballed her once more, so intensely Noelle shivered a bit. She was starting to feel like Sam could read her mind or something. "I'm coming from exactly the same place you both are," Sam said and it took Noelle a second to remember Jo had asked a question.

"Write this down, Jo," Sam continued, "because it will probably be the first and last time I ever admit it. Your clothes are perfectly fine. They're authentically you and you look lovely in them. Yes, even your logger jacket and rubber boots."

"Uh huh?" Noelle said, still unclear on where Sam was going with all this, but happy she wasn't being mean about Jo.

"'Authentically' me, hey?" Jo chortled. "Ooo-la-la."

Sam ignored her sister. "And Noelle, though your clothes are expensive and beautiful and much more my idea of fashionable, you often look stiff and uncomfortable. I'm shocked to say it, but you look way better in Cade's old shirt and cutoffs."

Jo nodded, though she looked reluctant to do so.

"You do seem happy and relaxed when you're outside working, regardless of what you wear. It suits you."

Noelle looked down at the pink rose she'd been admiring. It was a super hardy variety, one often spurned by serious rose gardeners precisely because of how unpretentious and easy to maintain it was. Stick it in dirt, any dirt, and it would grow and put on blooms all season. It was amazingly fragrant—and hardy to Zone 4. It could weather almost anything life threw at it.

"My clothes aren't my problem," she finally muttered. "It's these damn control top underwear."

There was a moment of silence, then all three of them started to laugh. From across the yard, Destroy-a-con howled at the injustice of being sidelined for all the fun.

Noelle plucked a rosebud from the transplanted rosebush and handed it to Sam. "It doesn't need a lot. Just put it in a glass bowl with some water and leave it alone. In a day or two, it'll be the most beautiful thing you've ever seen."

Sam smiled and Noelle brushed her hands on the thighs of her "matronly" pants. "Well . . . I should run. Lots to do today."

Jo and Sam nodded. At the edge of the lawn, Noelle wedged her feet back into her heels and departed.

Chapter 18

HALFWAY TO TOWN, NOELLE'S PHONE rang. She pulled onto the gravel shoulder to answer. After a minute or two of polite reassurances that it was "totally fine" and "quite all right" and "not to worry about it," she ended the call—but didn't resume driving right away.

Weird. Caren had been the one to initiate the lunch date in the first place, and now she was cancelling it on incredibly short notice. Noelle didn't mind. She'd said it was fine and she meant it, yet there'd been an off note in their conversation.

It had sounded like Caren was lying. She'd hesitated oddly before saying something unexpected had come up—and wasn't that the same excuse she'd given Jo regarding the girls' night? But why would Caren bother to lie? Noelle shook her head at herself. She was being ridiculous.

So what to do? She'd head to town as planned, of course, to pick up the few things Jo had requested. But then? An idea blossomed, followed by butterflies of anticipation. It was sort of sad when Noelle realized how foreign the excited feeling was, but at least she knew today's "prepare for a new life" task. And to her surprise, it ended up being fun—and taking most of the day.

Back at River's Sigh, she dropped off Jo's stuff first. The kitchen and dining hall were empty, so she put everything away and left a note. Then she fetched her own filled-to-bursting bags from the van and tried to sneak to Chinook cabin unseen. No such luck.

Jo cut her off, Callum in tow. And Cade. Darn it anyway.

"Thanks for shopping for me," Jo said cheerily, then stopped mid comment, noticing Noelle's loot. "Wow. Someone went shopping for herself too."

Cade's gaze was heavy on Noelle's face, then on the bags, then on her face again. Noelle felt herself flush and decided the best way to handle his presence was by acting like he *wasn't* present. It didn't work very well.

"I, uh, yeah . . . bought some new clothes," she admitted to Jo, eyes trained on the ground, wishing she could disappear into the hard packed dirt beneath her feet. What kind of ninny buys a whole new wardrobe just because two women she admires say her clothes are all wrong for her?

"Fun!" Jo said, like it hadn't had anything to do with her or Sam at all.

"You went shopping? All that stuff's new clothes?" Cade asked.

An awful thought hit Noelle. If she was leaving

him, she shouldn't be wracking up her credit card.

She bit her lip. "Yeah, is that okay? I'll probably return most of it. I just thought—"

Cade interrupted her babble. "It's fine, of course. It's nice. Did you get anything you liked?"

Noelle shot him a look, then shrugged. She had actually. She liked, no, she *loved*, all of it, even if it might look ridiculous on her. Each item, from the retro style swimsuit, to the gauzy skirts and open back shirt, and every other little thing, made her feel like her old self—her self from years ago. "I did. Thank you."

Jo cleared her throat and for an instant Noelle thought she was saving her from the awkwardness. But then Jo spoke, her face turning bright red as she did, and Noelle realized the reverse was true. Jo was throwing her to the wolves—or wolf—and totally knew it.

"So," Jo started. "Callum and I were wondering—"

"And I already said it was a great idea," Cade added, making Jo, if possible, turn an even deeper shade of maroon.

"If you guys wanted to do a camping trip the next few days, or more specifically, a tenting trip?" Callum finished.

What on earth? Noelle's brain stuttered. Cade agreed to camp, to sharing a tent, when they couldn't even bear to be in the spacious cabin at the same time? Before she could grunt some response, however, a huge black Hummer with lots of chrome and bumblebee yellow decals advertising a fitness club roared into the parking lot.

"What's *he* doing here?" Jo snarled. The venom in her voice shocked Noelle. She would've bet money Jo didn't harbor a hint of dislike for anyone. Apparently, seeing the daggers Jo's glare threw at the giant blond man in the driver's seat, it was money Noelle would've lost.

Callum moved forward as the man climbed down from the SUV, and Cade stepped closer to Noelle, like he too sensed the weird hostility rolling through the air.

"Heya, Callum." The blond grinned amiably at Callum's scowling face, then nodded toward Jo. "Heya, Jo."

"What do you want, Dave?" If Noelle hadn't seen Jo speak, she wouldn't have believed that cold voice came from her mouth.

"Ah," Cade whispered, more breath than volume— the sound of a connection being made. He ducked his chin and leaned in close. Noelle was unsteadied by memories from both the far past and the too-close-for-comfort near past. The sensation of him by her side was so ingrained in her psyche it was like part of her own skin, the scent of him, the warmth of his breath on her ear, the cotton whisper of his rolled cuff brushing her forearm . . .

Was she doomed to a forever of being so damn aware of him?

Sam's words drummed through her: *If you want him back, you could have him in a heartbeat.*

But she couldn't really. They could have wild sex, sure—and she'd given up pretending to herself that she wasn't still sort of addicted to him that way, but they couldn't have the true intimacy, the closeness, the oneness she craved—no, she needed. She couldn't bear being with him and constantly pining for him, knowing that she was just tiding him over until his next fling. How did anyone bear that? Maybe she should talk to Caren alone after all. Maybe she should call her and press her to set a new lunch date. Tell her how much she resented what she and Duncan had done to Cade, how they'd broken him and created a guy who thought that kind of relationship was acceptable. Could last. But then again, they'd proved it could, hadn't they? And maybe only Noelle saw the cost.

Cade purred in her ear, pulling her back to the confrontation in front of her. "That's Dave Holt. He and Callum used to be inseparable. I didn't believe Brian when he told me Dave tried to get with Jo himself by screwing Callum over, but there must be some truth to it. They're definitely not friendly now."

Understatement of the century, Noelle thought. Callum's fists were clenched by his sides, and his whole body was rigid.

"Oh, there he is. Hey, big fella," Dave crooned and moved toward Destroy-a-con. Noelle had missed whatever verbal exchange he, Jo and Callum had had, but she put two and two together pretty quickly.

"What? He's your dog? *You're* the owner?"

Dave turned and looked her up and down in a way that made her back stiffen. "Noelle, right? Pretty name for a pretty lady," he said. "You're with Cade, but you and I have met a time or two."

Noelle stepped back and darted a look at Jo, who shrugged but had obviously heard it too. Somehow Dave packed a lot of innuendo into his simple words—and it was ridiculous. If they'd met, that's all it had been, a cursory introduction at some family visit in the far past.

"Sorry, I'm bad with faces. I don't recall . . . "

"Well, yours is *very* memorable."

Who was this guy? Fortunately she didn't have to think of anything to say because Dave refocused on Destroy-a-con. "I'm sorry about all this," he said over his shoulder. "I was out of town and Hammer was staying with friends who live out here, but I guess he got lonely or wanted to be near the ladies. Can't blame the guy, can you?"

Ugh, Noelle thought. And *Hammer*? Seriously? Even Destroy-a-con was a legitimately better name than that.

"I'm just glad I got home before you guys took him to the pound or something. Can I pay you for the food and stuff?"

"No, it's fine," Noelle said. Destroy-a-con whined and lunged toward Dave, jumping and nudging his hand. Dave laughed. "Hey, fella. Down, *down*. It's okay. Let's go home, hey?"

Noelle breathed a little easier. Dave appeared to be kind to his pet, and the dog seemed happy to see him. Maybe Dave wasn't a total creep, after all.

"Actually, Dave, *I* have a bill," Jo said. "Your dog destroyed our yard and flowerbeds. We had to replant and—"

Dave crossed his arms and nodded sagely. "So finances are a bit tight, hey? Yep, little dreams like this are a tough go. Just send me an invoice—and make sure you add on something to cover the labor too."

Jo visibly blanched and Callum's eyes darkened. "It's fine. It was nothing," Callum said.

Dave shrugged. "Suit yourself, but you know where I work. If you need money, say the word."

Cade clapped a hand on Dave's shoulder and started him back toward his vehicle. "He will, man. Thanks."

Dave and his dog climbed into the Hummer and rolled out.

"Idiot," Jo muttered, then took Noelle's arm and tugged her away from the guys.

"About the camping trip idea. I'm really sorry. It was Cade and Callum's brainchild, a way to free up a cabin for Duncan's stupid friend. I don't really get it. Does Cade know you're leaving him? He seemed really into it and I tried to dissuade them, but at the same time, I didn't feel it was exactly my place to say,

'Hey, maybe your soon to be ex-wife doesn't want to sleep with you in such confined quarters.' I didn't know what to do."

It was quite a speech from Jo and Noelle felt for her. She and Cade had really put her new friend in an awkward position.

She patted Jo's arm. "It's fine. I don't know what Cade's up to either, but I'll make it work—especially if it helps you out."

"Are you sure?"

Noelle nodded.

Jo still seemed uncertain. "Okay then . . . and I guess it's good you agreed because I think he already told the girls you're all tenting and they're beyond excited."

Noelle had started to walk back toward the men. Now she froze. "What? He already told them?"

Jo shrugged apologetically. "I'm sure we could still change it—and for that matter, Callum and I have extra rooms. You could just move in with us, or maybe Duncan's friend could stay—"

"No," Noelle said with a vehemence that surprised her. "You and Callum are already doing enough for Caren and Duncan. I'll camp. It'll be fine."

And it would be fine, Noelle thought, gritting her teeth. She'd made a tactical error the other night, sleeping with Cade, alerting him to how wildly he still got to her—but despite how her whole stupid body hummed at the memory again now, she wouldn't make

that mistake again. Whatever game Cade was playing?
She was going to finish it.

Chapter 19

THEY DECIDED TO SPEND THE whole long weekend of the reunion at the campground for simplicity's sake, though Duncan's guest was only coming for the dinner party. As Noelle packed her and the girls' things for three days of camping, she realized she hadn't updated her Facebook page or contacted any of her friends since she'd left the city and it had been over two weeks.

"They're going to think I fell off the planet," she muttered, stopping mid-packing to grab her phone and take advantage of the cabin's Wi-Fi. The campsite would be off the grid.

She answered a few quick e-mails. Most people knew she was on holidays, so her inbox wasn't brutal. Raymond was the only one who didn't seem to understand it, actually—but delete, delete, delete solved that. Then she skimmed Facebook for a bit, commenting here and there and posting a happy birthday message to a woman she used to do yoga with. Last, she updated her status with a cheery note and a plug for Jo and Callum. It really was the least she could do. "Having the best time! Greenridge offers the most gorgeous getaway a busy city slicker could ever ask for. I'm even running around barefoot! Seriously!" She inserted a shocked looking emoticon, followed by a happy face. "And the food, ahhh, the food! I can't begin to describe it. Need some time away? Definitely put River's Sigh B & B on your list."

She logged out, powered off her phone and dragged all their suitcases to the front door. She'd round up Eva and Emily, put them on finding Cade duty with the instructions that they carry everything to the van while she did a quick weed check (she'd watered first thing, early, to avoid as much evaporation as possible), and then it should be all systems go.

Or not. The minute she stepped out onto the porch, shutting Chinook cabin's door behind her, it was crystal clear her plans were going to be interrupted. Cade and the girls were nowhere to be seen, but Sam was practically sprinting to her and Charlie's cabin, a panicked Jo on her heels.

"Sam, please. Wait. We'll figure something out."

"No." Sam didn't slow. "I can't—I won't be here. I'm a total idiot. I didn't even think."

"What's going on? What's wrong? Are you guys okay?" Noelle tore across the lawn and joined them on Silver cabin's porch just as Sam put her hand on the doorknob.

"It's a long story," Jo said wearily.

"It's a never-ending story, more like it," Sam corrected. "Called Sam-Is-Always-An-Idiot—the continuing saga."

Noelle lifted her hands in a mute question and looked from Jo's distraught face to Sam's. Noelle didn't know Sam very well, but she was still shocked by the difference in her. Sam, usually so cool, collected and seemingly invincible, was pale and trembling—though, from the set of her jaw, the shakes might've been from fury, not anxiety. Her green eyes were desperate and sparkled with—Noelle could hardly believe it—unshed tears.

"I mean, God, Jo. It's one thing for Charlie to know something academically, but to meet him, to see him in person? And Aisha? I know she's still on the fence about how she feels about me. This . . . it could make her hate me. And how could I blame her?"

"She already knows the story. And she knows, of course, it wasn't an immaculate conception. Of course, it won't make her hate you," Jo said.

Something akin to fear crawled through Noelle. "Meet who? See *who*? Did something happen to Aisha? Will it affect her custody of Mo somehow?"

"No." Sam shook her head. "It's nothing. I'm just being stupid."

More like you just came to your senses and realized you let your guard down with someone other than Jo, Noelle thought—and surprised herself by speaking. "False. It's obviously something. You're not the get fussed over nothing type."

"Do you even know me at all?" Sam said so dryly Noelle almost laughed out loud. After all, as she'd just established in her own head, she didn't really.

"I blow everything out of proportion," Sam continued. "It's kinda my thing, actually. Sort of like high heels are my signature footwear, freaking out is my go to—"

"Get off it, Sam," Noelle said, cringing a little at the smothery-mother tone of own her voice.

Miraculously Sam did as she was told, if a bit sarcastically. "Well, Noelle, since we were obviously talking to you and all, you might as well come in."

Noelle bobbed her head, held back another smile, and didn't waste steps.

Jo shut the door behind them and turned to Noelle. "Duncan's stupid last minute guest is Sam's old ex . . . Aisha's birth father whom she's never met."

"Seriously, Jo? You spill it just like that?" Sam slammed her keys on the counter.

"Whatever. You were going to tell her."

"Yeah, of course—but I'd at least draw it out a bit, add some drama. You make it sound almost . . . manageable."

"It *is* manageable," Noelle said. "Completely manageable."

"No, it's really not," Sam disagreed, her attempt to hide her anxiety in humor completely disappearing again. "He's a creep of the first order, and I've come a long way, Jo, but I can't face him. I'm sorry. I know

I'm putting you in a bind, but I can't. I just can't. I don't want to."

"You don't have to. Of course you don't have to," Jo said. "I already told you that and I meant it."

"You're planning to leave?" Noelle asked, catching on. "And that'll be hard on Jo because you were going to help out over the weekend?"

Sam nodded. "Nothing that would get my hands dirty, but you know . . . stuff that still needs a body. Play hostess at the big dinner on Saturday night. Emcee the talent show on Sunday night."

"There's a talent show on Sunday night?"

"Yeah." Jo nodded at Noelle, her brow furrowed. "And a renewal of vows Monday morning before everyone leaves. Didn't you read the itinerary for the weekend? I gave one to Cade, uh—"

"Never mind," Noelle assured her. "It's not important. What *is* important is making sure you have the help you need and that Sam doesn't have to entertain— or be entertainment for—Duncan and his disgusting friend."

"Wow, gurrl, you catch on quiiiick," Sam said. "We could learn something from you."

Noelle rolled her eyes.

"You don't have to be a bitch," Jo said.

Sam held up her hands in surrender. "I wasn't being bitchy, I swear. I was sincere. I'm happily surprised by how quickly she guessed Duncan and he-who-shall-not-be named are disgusting—"

"She's going to meet him. She might as well know his name's Rick."

"Oh, yeah, I guess. Everyone's going to meet him." Sam was instantly glum again. Sheesh, the woman's moods were hard to keep up with.

"I can stand in for you," Noelle said.

Jo shook her head. "You're camping—and Sam don't you dare say it again. Rick is not staying in Silver."

"But it's your most expensive unit."

"And it's your and Charlie's home away from home until your cabin is built—and you paid for it in full, in advance. Rick isn't going to taint it."

"Then maybe Noelle and Cade can—"

"No, we can't," Noelle interrupted. "The girls have their hearts set on tenting and I've reconciled myself to it. But that won't stop me from filling in for you. We'll all be coming here for most of the days and evening anyway for the reunion activities. It will be fine. My support underwear pack well."

They all laughed and the tension in the room ratcheted down slightly. Sam poured them each a glass of wine and held up her glass as if to toast, then frowned and lowered it. "You don't think it's weak or cowardly of me to take off, do you?"

Noelle and Jo shook their heads simultaneously.

"I'm usually the first one to run from any confrontation." Noelle bit her lip, then took a big inhale through her nose and forced herself to finish the thought. "It's one of my biggest flaws actually. I always suspect I'm in the wrong somehow or stupid or weak for thinking whatever I think—but in this case I stand by the idea that avoidance is the best policy. And I can't believe I'm saying this but Cade is actually right. Some things should never be discussed or dealt with in a public setting. I do think Aisha should be told he's coming—and who he is, though that's your call, of course, but the weekend's going to have enough drama without you having to meet someone you obviously wish could stay part of a long gone past."

"Well said. Ditto," Jo said.

"Ditto?" Sam echoed. "Jo, Jo, Jo . . . I expected something a little more sage from you, I admit."

Sam lifted her glass again. "Okay then. To the brave choice of fleeing!"

"To fleeing," Jo said with only slightly less enthusiasm.

Noelle raised her stemmed goblet too, but just smiled, didn't say the words. The whole thing had her thinking on fleeing. That was exactly what she was bent on doing, wasn't it? Fleeing to avoid confrontation and while she sympathized with herself too—or felt sorry for herself more like it—she couldn't help but feel that while the rationale behind Sam putting off a face-to-face with Rick was completely valid, her own intention to avoid, avoid, avoid until she could get home and pack and leave was, well, to borrow from Sam's analysis—a bit cowardly.

Sam chattered on about this and that, sounding chipper about doing a "mad pack" and "whisking Charlie away for a red hot weekend surprise"—but Noelle noticed that the worry lines by her eyes didn't relax and she gulped her wine, rather than sipped it.

Chapter 20

THE VAN WAS PACKED, AND the girls were buckled in and miraculously quiet. Noelle had stuck a movie on in the van's DVD player and they'd watched so little television the past two weeks, they were completely enraptured by the colorful noise. Before Noelle went off to find Cade, she cranked the air conditioning up out of habit—then realized the outside temperature wasn't as brain-melting as it had been. Perhaps sleeping in a tent wouldn't be pure torture after all.

She was rounding the corner of Jo and Callum's house, starting to get annoyed that Cade was nowhere to be found when it was his flipping idea to camp in the first place, when he came barreling out of the dining hall's door, his face a thunderstorm.

What now? she thought.

Cade halted the instant he saw her and his eyes narrowed. "Who the hell is Ray, and why is he leaving a message for my wife, asking to please have her call him back and to remind her he loves her?"

Noelle's stomach dropped. She was such a moron! Ray was so far from her mind these days she hadn't even thought of the potential ramifications of posting her whereabouts on Facebook. Of course the stalker had looked up River's Sigh B & B and found a phone number.

"I have no idea—" she started.

"Bullshit. He's that guy you were always going for coffee with, the one you said was just a 'friend.'"

"Well, yeah, but he was—"

"Bullshit!" Cade said again, much louder. "All this time you've been busting my balls about Sherry, and you've been carrying on with a guy who admits he's in love with you."

"But—"

"No buts." Cade grabbed her arm and pulled her toward Chinook cabin. After all, it would never do to have a fight or disagree around witnesses, right? They always had to look happy, happy, happy—no matter how deathly miserable and on the verge of collapse they actually were. He was such a hypocrite!

"I want to know what this 'another' chance is and I want to know now. What the hell was his first chance?"

Eva and Emily had spotted them through the minivan's big window and they watched their parents rush past with wide eyes. Their expressions stabbed Noelle's heart.

Cade released her arm inside the now empty Chinook and stood staring at her in the dim room, shaded from both the sun and any curious family by the heavy drapes they'd shut when they departed earlier. Even in the shadows she could see his hurt—and it kindled the rage she carried constantly these days into a roaring fire.

"How dare you? You, you—*asshole*. The only reason you're so sure I was cheating is because you were. You just can't entertain the notion that if the mighty Cade Archer fell so low anybody else could resist."

Cade snorted. Noelle raised her hand—and was instantly nauseated. What were they coming to? She was actually *what*? Tempted to slap him? To hit him? She dropped her hand, heartsick.

"We were just friends, like I told you repeatedly. All we did is talk. And when I realized he was hoping for more I was crystal clear that I wasn't in."

Cade's gaze faltered and he swallowed hard. The cold in his eyes had shattered somehow, but she couldn't fathom how or why. "There's more than one way to be unfaithful," he said slowly, as if working out some complex puzzle.

Noelle wanted to scream. It was so unfair. *He* was so unfair. "Are you kidding me?" she finally managed to whisper. "How can you be for real with this shit? Talking is intimate, yes—a form of connection, a basic human need. And if you think it's the same thing as me having sex with someone, well, bully for you. I'm going to have friends, not that it's going to be any of your business soon, and some of them will, surprise, surprise, be male. Deal with it."

"I don't care that you made a close friend. I'm happy you did. I know you need one, especially after . . . " His voice trailed off but they both knew he meant after losing Melissa.

Noelle's stupid body betrayed her and a burst of tears escaped. She brushed them away with angry jabbing motions. Cade turned slightly, like he didn't want to see her crying. "It's your not telling me about it that stinks like an affair. If it's on the up and up, why the secrecy?"

"There was no secrecy—and what the hell? You screw around on me, but I'm supposed to feel guilty because I met someone for coffee once or twice a week?"

Cade cracked his knuckles. The popping sound was almost violent. "I've told you over and over, it's not quite what you think."

The adrenalin surging through Noelle faded, and her fury dwindled to a soul-deep weariness. "And I keep asking *you* over and over, what was it then?"

Cade opened his mouth, then shut it again.

Pushing out the next words took excruciating effort. "What are we doing, Cade? We keep having the same battle and for what? We're done."

They stared at each other for a long minute. Noelle could feel emotions pouring off Cade, but couldn't bear to decipher them. He hated her. The thought should've made her relieved, but instead it gutted her. He moved first, striding to the door and throwing it open. The bright sky and sunshine was an assault.

"And anyway," she snarled after him. "You should bloody well know me better than that. I would *never* cheat on you. I might leave you but I wouldn't *cheat*."

His jaw dropped and his shoulders sagged like she had physically struck him. Obviously her words had hit some chord, but she had no idea what. For a second it looked like he was about to say something else, but in the end, he just shook his head and resumed his march to the van.

The DVD player blared from the backseat the whole way to the campground, but neither Cade nor Noelle told Eva to turn the volume down—not even when she cranked it higher still. It was as if they were all hoping to disguise the bitter silence oozing from the adults in the front.

Chapter 21

THE TINY CAMPSITE WAS ONE of two hundred interspersed through an old growth forest above a huge crystalline lake. Somehow, though, their graveled space still managed to feel private and remote, no doubt because of the massive trees, sprawling devil's club and other wild greenery that created a formidable border between itself and any other nearby campers.

Everything was more or less set up now and Noelle, who had crawled into the tent to change into her swimsuit at the girls' begging, exited the tent on her hands and knees, butt first—only to catch a glimpse of a shadowy presence out of the corner of her eye as she did so. Fantastic. She had company. Cade hadn't gone down to the water with the girls after all. His piercing eyes—which had obviously been on her backside—moved up her body as she, completely mortified by her awkward exit, got to her feet.

If he noted her discomfort, his voice gave nothing away. "Can we please try to make peace?"

How she wished for her beach towel, but it might as well have been miles away instead of draped over a lawn chair by the van. More naked than she ever liked to be in public, she felt worse than overexposed. She felt transparent.

He had a day's worth of stubble on his face and it was all she could do not to rub her hand—or her lips—along his rough jaw. And he was wearing baggy board shorts and nothing else. It had been ages since she'd donned swim attire, but it had been a long time since she'd seen him in swim shorts either. With embarrassment that bordered on horrified, she realized she was staring at the treasure line of silky hair that started at his naval and disappeared into the elastic waistband of his trunks. It was bizarre, but standing outside in the quiet pine scented air, it was almost like they were naked or something. Her stomach clenched. It wasn't fair. It really wasn't. That she would still want him so much when he didn't want her. She never, never, never should have slept with him the other night. Rather than helping her hormones to abate, it's like the activity had put them on high alert. It wasn't that hot here under the deep shade of the ancient hemlock and cedar canopy, but her body was aflame regardless. Don't let him be able to tell, she prayed. Please, spare me that one humiliation. Please.

Unable to meet his eyes a second longer, she shifted her gaze to the other two pup tents, also courtesy of Jo and Callum, decorating the shady site like bright red and blue mushrooms. Both girls had insisted on having their own tents and promised they'd be fine sleeping alone—which meant sharing with Cade in too close for comfort quarters again. The cabin was awful enough. The tiny tent wouldn't leave room for a body between them. Cade would be right there, pressed close to her all night. What was she going to do? What?

"So?"

It took Noelle a moment to register that Cade had spoken again. "So?" she repeated back dumbly.

Cade motioned around the campsite. "Can we put our fighting aside for a few days and let the kids enjoy this? Who knows if or when they'll get a chance to go camping again."

Noelle slid her feet into black flip-flops that lay just beyond the tent's yawning entrance. "Do you really think we're fooling them?"

"What do you mean?"

"The girls. You don't think they know we're nearing the end?"

Cade sighed heavily. "I don't know . . . I hope not."

Again, Noelle had to glance away. Why did he look so sad when he was the one who'd thrown the grenade into their marriage in the first place, then wouldn't even fess up to his part in it? "Okay," she relented. "Peace. But we should put everything out in the open and talk to them soon. Like on the drive home. They know something's up. How can they not? It's not fair."

Cade opened his mouth to speak, but two things

happened simultaneously, cutting him off and rendering them both speechless.

A huge snuffling blur bolted from a prickly stand of devil's club—completely undaunted by the hairy inch long thorns—and Eva and Emily came tearing into the gravel mouth of the campsite on bikes.

But they hadn't brought bikes.

And the beige and white blur reminded Noelle terribly of—

"Mom, Dad, look! It's Hammer. He's here with his owner, Dave," Emily exclaimed.

"We recognized him, Hammer, I mean, on the trail to the lake," Eva explained. "He knocked me down, but then Dave caught him and made him sit."

It didn't explain why the girls were on bikes.

As if cued, Dave jogged into the campsite. His hair was gelled and perfect and his deeply tanned skin gleamed. While it was a look that might appeal to some, Noelle thought it was too calculated to be truly attractive. Despite herself, her eyes went back to Cade's stubbled chin and tousled hair.

"And we meet again," Dave said. "Small world, hey?"

"It is," Cade agreed.

"Camping?" Dave asked.

"So it would seem," Cade replied dryly.

The two men exchanged a few more trivialities and while Dave's words were directed at Cade, his eyes seemed pinned on Noelle. But maybe that was delusional? She hoped it was.

"That's a knock out swimsuit on you, Noelle," Dave said when his and Cade's small talk lagged.

Noelle glanced down at herself. She had thought the one-piece was super cute, sort of Marilyn Monroe-ish or something, but between Cade's gawking earlier and Dave's ogling now, she wished she hadn't purchased it. She was probably hanging out all over the place. Why hadn't she put on a sarong or something?

She shook her head to dismiss his words. "I look fat." She didn't know why she said the words except that she felt them—not that that explained anything. She was usually good at keeping what she felt to herself.

Dave gave her such a concentrated up and down perusal that Cade actually stepped forward—and Noelle was happy that he did.

Dave, however, appeared oblivious. "Fat in all the right places, I'd say," he said cheerily, still studying her with open appreciation. It was mindboggling.

"Who's fat?" Emily asked, never content to be left out of a conversation for long. She rolled forward on the bike, feet on the ground, not on the pedals. "Hammer? He's not fat, he's just really big boned."

Noelle had to laugh.

Cade glowered. "Where did you get those bikes?"

Dave stepped forward. "Oh, that's me. Guilty as charged. I'd just finished up a beginner mountain bike class I'm instructing, and thought your kids might want to go for a spin."

"Well, here's the thing, Dave. You may know me, but you don't know my girls and I don't want you giving them anything, going anywhere with them, or pretty much talking with them without clearing it with me first. Got it?"

Dave held up his hands and looked at the ground. "I'm really sorry. I didn't think—I told them to ride here first and get permission to borrow them from you."

It was the first comment Noelle heard out of Dave that sounded sincere and not like he was trying to schmooze.

Eva cut a stern glare at her sister. "I told you," she said. "He's a stranger. We should've asked Mom and Dad *first*."

"That's right," Noelle said. "Make sure next time, if there is a next time, you clear any activity or gift with us before you accept."

The girls nodded and got off the bikes, glumly pushing them toward Dave.

"I didn't think he was a *stranger*-stranger," Emily stage whispered.

"Because you're an idiot," Eva said.

"Enough," Noelle cut her off. "You went along with it. It's not just Em's fault, and neither of you are in trouble anyway. I—we're—just reminding you."

"But you will be in trouble if you ever pull a stunt like that again. You know better." Cade motioned brusquely toward the purple and black mountain bikes. "Now get back on. I'll race you to wherever Dave's truck and trailer are."

The girls shrieked, clambered onto the bikes, and took off like shots.

"I'll meet you guys down at the lake for a swim before dinner," Noelle called after them.

Cade's eyebrows rose for a fraction of a second and both girls threw surprised looks over their shoulders. Oh, come on. It wasn't like she never joined in on recreational activities. From their expressions you'd think it was unheard of. She wondered if she was already losing them to their more fun parent when her and Cade weren't even living in separate houses, doing the single parenting thing yet.

Chapter 22

MAYBE IT WAS THE HOURS in the lake playing with the kids, then staying in his wet shorts and air-drying as evening deepened. Or perhaps it was because the campsite saw so little sun during the day that it cooled off all the quicker at night. . . . Whatever the reason, it was actually chilly. Cade didn't know the last time he'd been able to say that. Despite how painful sharing a tent with Noelle would be with her hating him more than ever, he was looking forward to his sleeping bag.

He said a final good night to the girls, each snuggled in her own solitary tent, then informed Emily again that no, Mom would not read her one last story. She'd read three already and it was late and she was already in bed.

The tent's zipper was loud in the shadowy blackness, and he wondered if he'd disturbed Noelle. As his eyes adjusted to the dark, however, he realized she wasn't asleep. Or even lying down. She was sitting upright, arms wrapped around her bent knees.

"Noelle?" he whispered. "What's up?"

She shifted and though he couldn't see her face, he

assumed she'd turned toward him. Her voice was congested. Like she was suffering allergies. Or like she'd been crying. "There's only one sleeping bag. You can have it."

He'd been about to dig into his packsack for a T-shirt and a pair of boxers because his not-quite-dry swim shorts were starting to chafe. Now he paused and tried to make out her expression, but it was futile. She was merely a darker shadow amid all the other shadows.

"That's ridiculous." It came out sounding accusatory before he could help it, but he was surprised that's all. "I packed the four sleeping bags you put by the door. I double-checked." Why did he default directly to defensiveness whenever he perceived she might be blaming him for something? He sighed. "I mean—"

"It's okay," she said. "It wasn't either of our faults. Just bad timing, bad luck, bad . . . everything, as usual."

Obviously, she was talking about more than just the sleeping bag. "I don't get it. How?"

"One of the sleeping bag rolls was just another inflatable sleep mattress. In its little nylon baggy thing, it looked like a sleeping bag. I just assumed—anyway, my bad. You can have the sleeping bag. I folded it out. It's unzipped for you."

"No, you can have it."

"No, Cade, it's fine."

"Seriously—"

"I said it's *fine*."

"But it's actually kind of cold."

No comment from Noelle.

"We could share."

A sniffing sound. Disgust or despair or just clearing her sinuses? Cade wasn't sure. A thought occurred to Cade and it made him sad which, him being stupid him, set off a spark of anger. "I won't touch you, if that's what you're worried about."

More silence. Fuck. They were ridiculous. The most frustrating idiots he'd ever met, in fact. But they'd been so good together once. It was unbearable to accept that they might never be again. And they'd used to be able to talk. She was the only person he'd ever really been able to talk to. *He used to talk to her, really talk to her.* The fact hit him like a kick in the gut. All this time he hadn't been able to figure out what to say, blaming her because she didn't intuitively know or understand his intentions and motives—but he was the one who had changed. Another thing she was right about.

Outside their un-cozy abode, the wind kicked up. A big pine branch clawed along the side of the tent.

He tried once more. "See . . . chilly."

Noelle sighed and he knew she'd given in. He was right.

"Okay," she said unhappily. "How about we unzip it all the way and use it like a blanket? And with double sleep mats, at least the ground will be soft."

Until she gave the very sensible solution, Cade didn't realize he'd been wholeheartedly envisioning—and obviously hoping—they'd be wrapped up in the close confinement of a sleeping bag together. Did he never learn? "Sounds good," he said even though it didn't.

The sleeping bag zipper whispered in the darkness and then there was a whisking-flapping sound as Noelle lifted the sleeping bag and shook it to settle flat.

Cade shucked off his swim shorts.

"What are you doing?" Noelle's voice was so panicked that Cade was startled.

"What do you mean?"

"You're not sleeping commando."

Ah, yeah, heaven forbid skin contact. It was interesting how intense she was about the not touching, no contact stuff. If she was really as done with him as she claimed to be, wouldn't that just be a given, not something she had to keep harping about?

Shadow-Noelle lay on her side and folded into a tight crescent shape. Cade sighed heavily. "Don't worry. I'm just getting out of my damp shorts. I plan to put on a hazmat suit."

Not a hint of a smile in her voice. "Good. And remember, no contact. You promised."

He didn't bother putting on a T-shirt after all. With both of them in it, the tent was warming up. He eased down beside her, careful to keep a good distance, and lay on his side too, facing the same direction she was. It was such an ingrained move on his behalf that he had to physically stop himself, mid-reach. He'd been about to put his hand on her hip and pull her close. How long had it been since they slept together? Actually *slept*? Sometimes he thought he missed that even more than regular sex.

"What are you doing?" she asked sharply. "Your hand moved."

Cade couldn't help it. He laughed sadly. "Shit, you caught me—but don't worry. I reined myself in."

Despite his reassurance and his promise, however, as the next tense minutes passed, he became increasingly aware of how thin his cotton boxers were—and how close he was to Noelle's curved form. Dammit. He wasn't going to sleep a wink.

If it's over anyway, you have nothing to lose, a voice muttered in his head. You might as well let yourself look like a jerk. You can't be any worse in her eyes as it is.

Cade considered that line of thinking—then nodded in the darkness. It was true. Worse case scenario he'd look like an idiot. She already thought he was one anyway. Besides, nothing ventured, nothing gained, right? And maybe, just maybe, she was extra vehement about him not touching her because she wanted nothing more than to touch him. His heart—and, if he was honest, his dick—leapt at the idea.

"I like your new bathing suit," he whispered.

Noelle didn't make a sound, but it was that, her extreme silence and absolute rigid stillness, that assured Cade she was awake, hadn't fallen asleep. Another tree branch scraped along the tent.

"You should show a bit of skin more often. It was all I could do not to grab you and kiss you."

Well, those words did the trick. Sort of. Just not the one he wanted them to. Noelle did make a noise. A snort. Unfortunately Cade didn't have any trouble interpreting her emotion this time. Complete scorn.

"I know you don't want to hear it from me, but you're beautiful. I'll always think so and I'll always want you."

"Uh huh." Noelle's voice was so quiet, Cade would've thought her response was just his imagination—except if it was his imagination she would've rolled over, said "Omigod, me too," and jumped him.

"It's true."

"Cade, you promised."

"Promised not to touch you—and I'll keep that promise as long as you want me to. I didn't promise not to talk to you though—or not to think about touching you."

"Come on, give me a break," she whispered, sounding strangled. "*Please.*"

"Mmmm, *please*, hey? As we established not that long ago I do like it when you beg. Please what? Please rub my hand along your soft, glorious—"

"*Cade.*" It was like she was trying to sound stern,

but her voice was still velvet soft.

"Thigh," he finished.

She inhaled sharply.

"You sound surprised I said thigh." He leaned in closer. "What did you think I was going to say, your soft glorious *what*?"

Noelle laughed lightly and Cade's heart sped.

"Or maybe you were saying please grab your gorgeous fat-in-all-the-right-places body and—"

Noelle froze. "Really?" she said finally. "You use that creep's line?"

"Well, uh, you turned pink when he said it. I thought you liked it."

Noelle shifted and folded her pillow then jammed it more securely under her cheek. Damn!

A second later she confirmed the moment was lost, though her voice remained sense-stirringly soft. "Did you do this with Sherry too?"

Cade rubbed his forehead wearily. Everything always came back to that, didn't it? Sherry, Sherry, Sherry. Would Noelle ever let up?

"Do what?" he asked before he caught himself.

"Make her feel like you genuinely cared? Like you wanted her, only her?"

Cade pushed his clenched fist against his mouth, punishing himself. Outside, the wind blew harder. Leaves or twigs skittered over the roof of their shelter. He was trying to formulate some kind of answer, when something rustled loudly outside the tent door and the zipper toggled.

"Who's there?" Noelle called.

"Mama?" Emily's voice, timid and shuddery, carried through the paper-thin wall.

"Mom?" Eva seconded, sounding equally scared. "Someone's trying to get into our tents. Can we sleep with you guys? Please?"

Cade was already in motion, feeling for the main zipper, as Noelle said, "Of course, sweeties. Dad's getting the door right now."

And then the girls were piling in like puppies, clumsy and sniffling, tripping over themselves and the sleeping bags they'd dragged with them.

"Shh, shh," Noelle said. "It's okay. You're okay."

Cade rummaged for a flashlight and flicked it on. He studied his daughters' faces in the dim beam—tear-stained and pale—then took in Noelle in her soft stretchy tank top and baggy cotton shorts, comforting their babies that weren't babies at all anymore. His guts churned with a convoluted mixture of happiness and fear and impending loss. She'd put an arm around each daughter and was clucking to them the way she had when they were very small, whispering in each of their ears, teasing them and reassuring them all at once. He caught a few words. "Just the wind, no monsters, I promise."

Noelle glanced over suddenly, by chance meeting his gaze. Her eyes widened and she looked stricken. She swallowed as if to say something, then shook her head and resumed her crooning. Cade caught one more reassurance. "Don't worry. No boogeyman will come near with your Daddy here."

"Because he loves us and will always keep us safe, right?" Emily asked sleepily, and Cade felt a swell of relief. At least his daughters heard and retained some of the positive things he said, too.

"More than anything in the world, munchkin," Noelle agreed.

Soon the girls were tucked in, one on either side of him and Noelle, and were pretty much out for the count. Noelle looked at Cade, then rolled her eyes and shook her head. He wasn't fooled though. She loved these moments when they still needed her, needed *them*, the way they had when they were tiny. His heart was breaking.

She returned to the position she'd held before they were interrupted—on her side, facing away from him. He studied the curve of her shoulder where it smoothed into her neck and wished he could kiss it, then he clicked out the light. He shuffled over the best he could to make room for her, but it was a small tent for two, let alone four. His body framed hers and he wished for the millionth time that he hadn't taken the shelter they found in each other for granted. He tried to move back some more. There were inches between them, at best.

"It's fine," she whispered. "Don't worry."

His hand lifted with a will of its own again, then hovered, uncertain. His want—his need—was a terrible, wrenching thing.

"Noelle," he whispered.

"Yeah?"

"May I rest my hand on your hip? Please."

A heartbeat's pause, then, "That would be touching me."

"I know."

He thought he felt her nod in the darkness, but he didn't move. Then shock coursed through him, followed by pleasure. She reached behind herself and took his hand in the darkness and placed it on her waist. He exhaled and hooked his thumb into the waistband of her shorts. His palm rested against the softness near her belly, and he splayed his fingers wide, encompassing her hipbone and the crease where her torso joined her leg, wanting to hold as much of her, all of her, that he could.

At first, she was tense, but soon she softened. She arched her back more deeply, pressing her rounded backside into his pelvis. Spooned together, they were a perfect nestled fit. He hardened, couldn't help it, but he knew it was okay. It was like old times. A bedroom full of thwarted desire because the kids were sprawled everywhere and, this time at least, he wouldn't have changed it for anything. The back of his eyes and his throat itched, and he was glad for the darkness.

Her arm overlapped the one of his that held her, and her hand lightly cupped his fingers on her hip. Sleep would be a long time coming, but he didn't care.

In fact, he almost wished he wouldn't doze off. He didn't want to miss a second of this.

Her breathing grew soft and even and he suspected she was sleeping, but he took the chance anyway.

"And the answer is no," he whispered against her silken hair. "No, I didn't do that with her. And no, I never made her feel like I cared or wanted her— because I never did. I only ever wanted you. Everything else was a mistake and I'm sorry. I'm so sorry."

Noelle shifted against him, and her breath hitched, making a soft, slightly sad sound. He didn't know if it was a coincidence, if maybe she wasn't asleep after all. He closed his eyes and wished and wished.

Chapter 23

THE LAKE WAS A SAPPHIRE blue expanse, glinting and shimmering in the early morning sun as far as the eye could see, then melting into the mountains on the horizon—mountains that were shade after shade of blue, soft and dreamy in the distance. Noelle thought about the abundant beauty in the world and in relationships, thinking of her sweet girls and Cade's tenderness toward them and, seemingly, last night, even to her. Then she flashed to the ugliness that so often roiled between them.

She couldn't decide if the mystery and extreme beauty of life made the hard parts more bearable—or if the opposite was true. If knowing what beauty and goodness existed, within nature, within people, within families, made the ugliness, loss, and failings harder to deal with.

She took a deep breath of the earthy air and sipped her coffee, infinitely glad that she'd sneaked down to the beach alone, letting Cade and the girls clean up the remains of breakfast.

The stretched out pajama bottoms she'd pulled on

when she climbed out of the tent bagged around her ankles, damp from the dew in the grass on the trail, and her loose hair was probably a mess, but she didn't care. In the late hours of the night, wrapped in Cade's strong arms, half asleep and half dreaming, she'd kept returning to the expression she'd glimpsed on Cade's face as she'd calmed the girls. It didn't fit with the beliefs she had about him—or her convictions about what he thought about her. She'd arrived at some deep awareness that she needed to stop giving so much attention to outer appearances—and focus on what was going on internally, for herself and others. And it had her rethinking her decision to just leave, no matter what.

She very well might leave Cade. She'd meant what she'd said. She wouldn't stay with someone who didn't love her. Or with someone who even might love her, but was unfaithful. And it wasn't just ego. It was for her girls. She couldn't model that for them as they grew older and came to understand those kinds of dynamics. But something was up. Yes, Cade was an incompetent oaf when it came to expressing himself, but he wasn't that good a liar. There was no way he could feign such a tender look—and no reason he would try to, especially when he had no clue that she'd look up when she did. And then there was his confusing apology when he thought she was asleep.

She wasn't going to take his words as God's truth or anything, but she was going to dig into them. He, even speaking in the cover of night, thinking she might not hear him, sounded guilty and tortured as he assured her he had never treated Sherry the way he treated her. That everything had been a mistake. But he still wasn't clear about what the mistake was. His cheating? Or her thinking that he'd cheated? She was going to get to the bottom of it and make her decision from an educated place, not an emotional one.

She etched a large curve in the sand with her bare foot, then realized it looked like half a heart. How fitting. That's how she felt being with Cade but not *being with him*. Half-hearted. It was time to fix that.

She tried to ignore the tiny fire of hope the decision kindled. Her decision to leave him, her vow to, always made her feel helpless and angry. By contrast, this decision—to give him the benefit of the doubt and to try to make a way for him to really talk and for her to really hear him out—made her nervously optimistic.

What kind of pain was she letting herself in for now? And was she fooling herself? Was she falling prey to the same type of self-delusion Caren must suffer in order to stay with a husband who was a habitual cheater?

Suddenly Noelle shrieked. Something large and black dove toward her, screaming and chortling.

She ducked, covering her head with her hands, then looked up. A massive black crow was beating the air in a frenzied panic, squawking. Something metal, flashing silver and gold, dangled from its black claw-footed leg. Noelle's brain made the connection. It had snagged some kind of fishing lure, was caught in fishing line. Poor creature.

The bird landed on the sand an arm's length away, and shook itself frantically. There was a tinny jingle and the lure—still attached to the bird—landed near Noelle's bare feet.

Before she could consider her actions, Noelle leapt forward, snatched the lure and pulled—then zigzagged, changed directions, and pulled some more. The bird made a weird chattering sound and propelled itself backwards. There was resistance, then the line drew taut and let go. Noelle stumbled a little. The crow shot up into the air, hovered as though still ensnared, then flapped its wings and recognized its freedom. Cawing twice, it zipped across the beach then flew back, remaining low, as if waiting for her to say something.

"You're welcome," Noelle called. The bird chortled and cawed a few more times, then flapped out of sight behind a huge bank of evergreens. Noelle considered the silver and gold bangles spooned together in her hand.

Chapter 24

River's Sigh was a different place. The circular parking area was packed with vehicles and the grounds swarmed with people.

"I don't think it would matter if I hadn't fixed up the flowerbeds," Noelle said as Cade looked for a place to park the van. "There are so many bodies, I don't think anyone can see the grass, let alone the flowers."

"Yeah, it's ridiculous," Cade agreed, looking tense. "And I think you're right. We shouldn't have come. We should've just sent a card. It's a sideshow."

Noelle shrugged as she too took in the huge blue and white awning that formed an entertainment hall where a live band was setting up and a bouncy castle for kids that was almost inflated. What could she say? It *was* a sideshow. A total circus. She wondered if Jo had known about the band and the bouncy castle. She hadn't mentioned it if she had.

In the backseat, Emily craned her head this way and that, oohing and ahhing—and Noelle finally thought of something to say.

"Hey." She touched Cade's forearm. "You wanted this holiday because it would be special for the girls—and it will be. It will be amazing. Who else has grandparents who bring in carnival rides for their anniversary?" She motioned toward a semitrailer and a group of men who seemed to be unloading an honest-to-goodness carousel.

Cade pulled to a stop beside a big camping trailer, turned sideways in his seat and studied her. "You're right," he said slowly, then nodded. "Thank you."

The girls undid their seatbelts and bolted from the van as soon as they were given permission. Cade and Noelle stayed put a minute.

"What about for us?" Cade asked softly. "Will this holiday be memorable for us, too?"

Noelle's heart pounded. It undoubtedly would be, but for good or bad? Was it the end of them or something else? She bit her lip, wanted to say . . . what? She didn't even know. And she had too much to help Jo with to have this conversation now.

"Well, that remains to be seen, doesn't it?" she asked, aiming for a light tone. A shadow of hurt darkened Cade's eyes. "I want it to be," she confessed. "I really do—and memorable in a good way. And I've been reconsidering some things I told you were set in stone, but don't get too excited. Nothing will change if you don't talk. I mean really talk."

Cade studied her so intently that she shivered under his unreadable gaze. Then he nodded. "Okay. Okay."

THE REST OF THE DAY passed in a blur. Once everything was set up, there was an official meet and greet. Then a scavenger hunt. Dinner was a potluck followed by a dessert bar. The kids were beyond wired with excitement all day and crashed the instant they got back to the campsite. Noelle was equally exhausted and when she climbed into the tent only to find them sprawled out in it again, she was too wiped to insist they sleep elsewhere. For the second night in a row, they slept like a family of puppies, all piled together. Her bone deep tiredness didn't have the one effect she'd hoped for, however. Despite how weary and out of it she felt, she wasn't too tired to be aware of Cade's log-like presence behind her and how she liked it. Craved it.

Eva had already dropped off, when Emily mumbled happily, "We're like bugs in a rug, hey, Mom?"

A comfortable blanket of silence descended, but when their youngest snored once, Cade whispered in Noelle's ear, utterly quiet to ensure their daughters wouldn't hear. "If that's true, I think I'm a stick bug." He tugged Noelle's hips, snugging her butt against him tighter, so she'd have no questions about what he meant.

It was so corny it shouldn't have been a turn on in the slightest, but the nights of close quarters had been torture on her libido. She bit back a giggle despite herself. "Shh."

He wouldn't.

"We need to ditch the kids tomorrow, ladybug. Get them set up in their own tents again. Just saying." His voice was almost imperceptible, but his mouth was so close to her neck she could feel his words. "Wanna?"

Did she ever.

"Hmmm," she said noncommittally.

He ground against her lightly. Shit, shit, shit.

"I know what you're doing," he murmured again.

He knew what *she* was doing?

He spoke once more, this time feigning a terrible Russian accent. "You have ways of making me talk."

Talk. Right. Exactly. It was good one of them remembered.

"Good night, Cade."

He chuckled, sounding all too pleased with himself. "Night, Noelle."

Noelle drifted off to sleep with happy thoughts, planning to bring the weird fishing thing she'd taken from the crow to Jo to find out what it was, letting herself imagine good things for her and Cade, and thinking more and more that she had misunderstood everything and that they did indeed have some sort of future together.

Because she was a brain dead idiot, that's why—as Saturday reminded her loud and clear.

Chapter 25

THE MORNING DAWNED HOT AND hazy, though again
the campground shielded them from the reality of what
the temperatures were going to be later in the day. And
as they rolled back into River's Sigh for day two of the
Family-Reunion-Slash-Anniversary-Party, once more
the girls were out of the van almost before the tires
stopped moving.

Noelle and Cade both heaved big sighs as they
reached for their door handles, a fact that made them
share a wordless smile of commiseration.

So far, so good—the mood of the past two days
prevailed. And then Noelle was reminded of the truth
of their situation, not just her wishful thinking, and
their fledgling peace blew to hell.

Cade was making his way across the lawn in front
of her when a high-pitched squeal of feminine ecstasy
split through the hum of small groups of chatting
people.

"Cade? Omigod, it is you. *Cade!*" An eight-foot
blonde, all legs and breasts and impossible curves on
her skinny frame came flying across the gravel and

wrapped herself around Cade, burrowing herself in his neck.

To give Cade credit, for his part he looked completely stunned, hands at his sides, not hugging back, staring over the cooing woman's head, seeking Noelle's eyes with a pleading look.

She raised her eyebrows. "Let me guess . . . somehow I don't get the feeling she's a cousin." She hoped desperately that the dry note in her voice masked what the scene was revealing to her. That she was dumb. That Cade was who he was—and women would always flock to him. And she was who she was, a woman whose body had seen better days and whose personality seemed to have reset itself to depressed and morose. Like it or not, and whether it was his conscious intention or not, he'd stray, he'd stray, he'd stray . . . the hated fear cycled through her head again and again.

The woman had stopped hugging him—but now, if anything, her touch seemed even more intimate. She was holding each of his hands loosely in hers, staring up at him like there was no one else around. "God, I never hoped in a million years . . . " Just what she'd "never hoped" was left up to Noelle's best guess because she trailed off and took a deep, appreciative inhale. "Mmm, you even smell the same."

Noelle wanted to shrink into the ground. When exactly had this bombshell known her husband? Was she one of the "old friends" he'd visited previous vacation years? The crowd had gone quiet and stood staring. Noelle knew they were each thinking the same thing.

She noticed Cade was trying to yank his hands away, but the woman just gripped him more tightly.

Shockingly, it was Caren, of all people, who came to the rescue. She pushed through the crowd and placed a paint-stained hand on the woman's shoulder—a detail that caught Noelle by surprise, despite the situation and her stress. The formal party was tonight and Caren had paint all over her? Maybe she was planning to duck out later to get ready.

Paint and grubby clothes notwithstanding, Caren's voice was done up to the nines, as cold and cultured as Noelle had ever heard it. "Get a grip, Rae-Anne. You dated my son in high school—and you married someone else. Let's not pretend you have anything more between you than there is. It's beyond pathetic, dear."

"I just wanted to catch up. I've never forgotten you, Cade. Who would?" Rae-Anne's voice was quieter now at least, though what she was saying still felt like hot lead pouring itself over Noelle's back.

Cade was smiling and shrugging and backing away. "Nice to see you again, Rae. You're looking . . . good."

"Oh, thank you. I just returned from a week at a spa, actually."

Noelle was halfway to the dining hall, desperate to start on food prep with Jo, anything to distract her from the rage and sorrow billowing through her.

Cade caught up to her by the side door to the kitchen, inconveniently private and out of view. She couldn't even say "Not here, not now" to him.

"Noelle, come on. She's a crazy ex-girlfriend—from when I was kid, for crying out loud."

"I know that . . . now." She sighed and felt so, so, so terribly weary. "But I believe her."

"What do you mean 'believe her'? Believe her about what?"

"That she's just one in an almost unending list of women who'd drop their panties for you in a red hot instant if you smiled at them."

"But you're the only woman I want dropping her panties for me—even your big weird grandma ones."

The attempt to make her smile failed dismally. If anything it reopened an old wound and triggered fresh blood. The pain was almost physical. Noelle crossed her hands over her heart and bowed her head. "And I don't believe you."

"But—"

"We keep coming back to the same thing over and over again, Cade. And I saw you. *I saw you.*" In that second, she relived the scene that had been torturing her for months and months: going to surprise Cade at his office, him, drunk, stumbling out before she could even knock, his shirt untucked and unbuttoned, his tie missing, his hair ruffled like he'd just had sex, and lipstick smudged on his swollen mouth. Even with all that though, the most damning thing was the smell—

the expensive-but-trashy candy sweet perfume emanating off him—and off the scantily clad PA who appeared in his office doorway seconds after he'd exited it.

"Cade," she'd called. "We only just got started, come and—" Then she noticed shell-shocked Noelle and rushed to say something else, but Noelle didn't hear what it was, couldn't make sense of it—a feeling she related to again as she listened to Cade now.

"You think you saw me. Or you think you know what you saw," he said miserably.

"Yeah, yeah, I do," she said. "And obviously I'm right because you've never given me one shred of explanation or evidence or anything to prove different-ly, or even to show that she was the first one or the first time—"

The kitchen door opened and Jo rushed out—then stopped in her tracks when she saw them. "Noelle, Cade, hello and thank God! I was praying reinforce-ments would arrive." Her cheerful voice petered out. "Oh . . . uh, you guys look like it's important. Take all the time you need. I'm fine. No worries."

Noelle shook her head, smiling sadly. "Don't be silly. I was already on my way."

Cade caught her hand as she brushed past him. She stopped mid-stride and stared down at his clasping fingers without speaking until he broke his hold on her and stepped back.

Chapter 26

CADE GUESSED THE TINY WHITE lights wound through the trees were pretty, but it all reminded him of his and Noelle's wedding so much that he wanted to retch. And the rumble of small talk and laughter—of obvious happiness and lightheartedness—was equally unbearable. He'd eaten the five-course meal without tasting it, shoveling it into his mouth only because he didn't want to stand out by not eating. He'd managed to sit beside Noelle without breaking down or flying into a helpless rage. Why did being powerless make him so damned angry? She picked at her food, unusual for her, but other than that gave no sign of being upset. Her opening greeting and toast to the assembled dinner party had been charming and light beat. Maybe their conversation that afternoon hadn't swayed her. Why the hell had Rae-Anne had to show up anyway? If he'd known Duncan was going to invite the whole town he wouldn't have come. He'd honestly thought it was a *family* reunion, a get-together with the sole purpose of reconnecting everyone again. He was a moron. Of course, Duncan would use it as a way to show off his money to all of Greenridge.

"Speech, speech," someone called. Around the room, a boisterous tinkling of silverware on glasses commenced. Noelle stood, smiling, and made her way back to the front of the outdoor dining room.

"You were reading my mind," she said into the mic. "But it won't be me speaking. We have the lovely couple themselves who'd like to say a few words—but first, while they're making their way up here, can I get a big round of applause for that amazing dinner and for all the work Jo and Callum and their staff have done to create such lovely celebration weekend?"

There was a roar of enthusiastic clapping and cat-calls. When the room quieted, Duncan and Caren were up at the podium.

Cade studied his parents and wondered what he should feel. How did other people feel about their parents? He felt . . . removed. All he'd ever wanted was to be cared about, to know they'd forgiven him for being the reason they'd "had to" get married, but as ever, they were so wrapped up in their own lives, happily or sadly, he was out of the loop of their concern in any real way. He thought of how he felt about his daughters. Had his parents ever felt that way about him?

Duncan was grinning like a politician and took the microphone from Noelle as if he'd been waiting to do so all night long. He probably had been.

Before Duncan spoke, he put his arm around Noelle, pulled her close, then wrapped his hand around her wrist and held her arm up like he was introducing a prizefighter.

"And thanks to my eldest son's gorgeous wife for emceeing on the fly, too. Look at her. My boy might not be the sharpest tool in the shed, but he knows how to pick 'em, hey?"

There was another smattering of applause, weaker than the first.

Noelle's smile froze, and though he suspected no one else could tell, Cade knew it was all she could do to keep standing there. She wasn't a touchy feely person—well, except for with him and that was likely past tense now too.

Cade listened to his father at first, he really did— but when his speech turned out to be a longwinded recitation of accomplishments and victories, he tuned out and turned inward, realizing something insane. He'd genuinely thought his talk with his father at the stupid stag night had gotten through to him. He'd actually been expecting his father to apologize to his mother, to say that after thirty-five years he finally realized what he had with her and that he'd taken her for granted and was sorry. To say he loved her, appreciated her, was going to live differently . . .

Cade bowed his head. He was having difficulty breathing.

Did every kid spend their whole life, regardless of how old they grew, wishing their parents would get it together? He darted a glance at Eva and Emily. They were both sitting straight-backed, politely listening. What was going through their heads? It was a sad shock to him that he had absolutely no clue. They were so young, yet they'd already learned the Archer trait well. They could veil their emotions like champs, even Emily who was by nature an open book.

"To you, my dear," Duncan called out boisterously, lifting his glass to the crowd, more than to his wife.

"Hear, hear," the guests chanted back.

Caren took the microphone from Duncan with a wan smile. She looked more resigned than celebratory, and her expression was as familiar to Cade as the color of her eyes or the texture of her hair. Had she ever taken joy in him or his brothers as transparently as Noelle did in their girls? And if she had, was it marriage to Duncan that grinded it out of her?

"Thank you all for coming," Caren started, and unlike when his father commenced blathering, Cade found himself holding his breath in anticipation of whatever she'd say. With Duncan he'd—they'd all—heard it a billion times. With Caren . . . well, she hardly ever spoke. Not really. "And I'm sorry to dump this on you in public, as it will no doubt come as a surprise . . . but I've been trying and trying to do it privately to no avail." She withdrew a manila envelope from under her arm. Cade hadn't noticed it wedged to her body. "Duncan and I, as he pointed out, have accomplished a lot—and I will try not to waste too much time on regrets, though in how I raised our sons, it will be difficult."

It felt like she was speaking directly to Cade and her eyes pinned his.

"And I apologize for this farce of a celebration, though I hope you enjoyed visiting one another."

You could have heard a pin drop. What was she getting at? Surely not what the growing pit in Cade's stomach suggested . . .

"Duncan and I are getting a divorce. Our son Brian will be handling the details."

The room made a collective gasping sound. Cade's mind reeled and he swayed unsteadily in his chair. This couldn't be happening. It couldn't be. And she was getting Brian to handle it? What kind of parent pitted her child against their other parent?

His mother was speaking again, cutting his thoughts short.

She raised her glass high and met Duncan's flushed, shocked face with an expression that was almost apologetic. "To you, Duncan. You cold-hearted, selfish, chronically unfaithful bastard."

"This is nonsense," Duncan sputtered.

Caren's eyebrows spiked upwards. "Nonsense I've been informing you of for months, but just like every day in our thirty-five years together, you couldn't be bothered to hear me or take me seriously."

"You aren't serious. Of course you aren't."

It was like there was no one else in the room.

"Oh, I'm serious all right. Like a big goddamned heart attack."

Cade had never heard his mother use a cliché before, let alone say goddamn. Then he realized what she was doing. She was quoting Duncan. Mocking him by using a phrase he favored. It was too much. Everything was too much.

He stumbled to his feet, mumbled something incoherent to the girls about being back in a minute, and pushed past the people seated near him. He tried his best not to step all over them or trip on their outstretched legs, but was completely unaware of whether he succeeded or not.

Chapter 27

OVER THE HEADS OF THE stunned guests and through the shadows cast by the flickering candles and glittering strands of white lights, Noelle saw Cade bolt. Then, in the time it took for her to quickly excuse herself to Jo and ask her to keep an eye on the girls, he disappeared.

Outside the perimeter of the party's lights, the darkness seemed deeper—yet she was only minutes behind him. How far could he have gone? He wasn't in the van. Or the main dining hall. The kitchen was empty too, except for Aisha up to her elbows in a sink of sudsy water, scrubbing pots and pans. Her baby Mo, as ever, was nearby on the floor, banging two pot lids together like cymbals.

"Is everything okay?" Aisha asked when she saw Noelle's face.

Noelle shook her head, hesitated, then figured it would be common knowledge sooner or later, so there was no point holding back. "Caren used her toast tonight to notify Duncan that she wants a divorce."

Aisha's head jerked and her eyes widened. "For

real?"

Noelle shrugged. "That's what she says. . . ."

Aisha pulled the drain on the sink and there was a slurping belch as the water started to drain. "This family almost makes me and my mess feel sane."

Noelle looked down at Mo who dimpled up at her, then slammed the noisy lids again.

"No, no," Aisha quickly corrected Noelle's misunderstanding. "Mo's not my mess. She's the only thing I've gotten right in a long time. I just wish there was a way to get rid of my scuzzy ex that wouldn't involve jail time."

Noelle nodded, but glanced toward the door, torn. Cade had looked decimated—but she really did feel for Aisha, though she only knew a little of her story. And then she recalled Duncan's last minute guest: Rick-whoever-he-was. Had Aisha met her birth father then? She seemed remarkably unfazed if she had.

Aisha followed her gaze. "Oh, you're really worried about Cade? I'm sorry. I'll quit blathering."

"You're not 'blathering' at all—"

"Go," Aisha said. "My complaints, unfortunately, will keep."

Noelle nodded. "I want to hear them though. Rain check?"

"You bet."

Aisha sank down beside Mo and tapped out a rhythm on the floor as Noelle departed. Mo gurgled with glee and clanged the pot lids again.

Noelle checked Chinook cabin just in case. It was quiet and dark—and looked uninhabited, which was a bit weird. She wasn't expecting Rick and his family to be there. They'd be at the dinner obviously, but she'd thought they'd have left a light on or something. She stood alone on the path, unsure of what to do, where to look. Cade would be devastated by the evening's reveal because as much as she'd disagreed with him, Cade had always held onto his childhood hope that deep down his parents loved each other.

Over the years, Noelle had tried to talk about other reasons couples sometimes stayed married, reasons that had nothing to do with love, but he wouldn't hear it. Caren's voice rang in her memory, *just like every day in our thirty-five years together, you couldn't be bothered to hear me or take me seriously*, and she corrected herself out of fairness to Cade. He heard her, even asked questions, just never could bring himself to believe the worst about his parents. Or, for that matter, about themselves, their marriage.

Where was he?

An idea struck her, and although she didn't want to walk into the forest alone, she did anyway. The pine needles under her feet were tinder dry and as she got further away from River Sigh's main grounds and the murmur of voices grew fainter, the sounds of the forest magnified. A large scuffling sound made her freeze, heart pounding. Was it a bear? She laughed nervously when a huge toad rustled out of the crunchy underbrush and onto the path. Good grief, it made a lot of noise for a small creature.

Then, finally, the cabin Cade and Callum had been working on loomed into view, a light gray monster rising out of the tree line and into the ink black sky. She picked her way to the side of the building, wishing Cade had brought Callum to talk with, so she'd have a chance to eavesdrop and get some clue about what was going on inside his head and why he'd taken off.

As she came around the corner, she scanned the deck for a shadow or lump that might be Cade, and her intuition proved flawed. It was empty.

She turned away, defeated. Obviously he didn't feel the need to talk. He probably didn't want her company. Maybe she shouldn't have tried to seek him out in the first place.

A shadow shifted against a tree, and a hand reached toward her from the darkness. She shrieked and jumped back.

"Sorry," Cade said, no hint of laughter in his voice at startling her so badly. "I thought you saw me."

"Well, you thought wrong." Noelle moved to the deck, hoisted herself up, then sat on the edge, legs dangling. Cade joined her and for a few minutes they stared up at the sky in silence. In the moonlight, Noelle saw silvery tracks on Cade's face, like he might have been crying and her heart wrenched.

"Are you all right?" she whispered.

He shrugged, then broke his silence. "I get it now,"

he said flatly. "Don't worry."

"What do you mean?"

"That—my parents—that's us too, right? That's what you were always trying to say, that you knew they were a farce, even if I didn't."

Noelle could only shrug.

"And you know we'll end the same way. That's why you don't want to keep trying. Why prolong the inevitable?"

Noelle clenched her fists so tightly that in the silvery glare of the moon her knuckles shone white. She should just agree with Cade now while he was so quietly resigned. They could stop all the misunderstandings and pain they kept inflicting on each other and the kids.

"It doesn't have to be like that for us," she said, her voice breaking with relief that she'd actually said the words out loud, expressed her hope for better or worse. "Or maybe it doesn't anyway."

Cade turned toward her, but kept his eyes downcast. "I don't know what you're saying."

She put her hands on either side of his face and lifted his gaze to meet hers.

"I always felt like what we had was too good to be true—that you were too good to be true."

Cade snorted.

"Shh, let me finish. So maybe this is partly my fault. Maybe by worrying you'd stray, by always being certain that I wasn't enough to keep you interested in the long haul I sort of pushed you into—well, you know. And then, after Melissa, I withdrew—"

"Stop—"

"No, *you* stop. Let me finish."

Cade huffed, but did as asked.

"But I always promised myself—and I meant it and still mean it: I would never be with a man who hit me or the kids or who cheated. What I didn't know was how hard it would be to leave. As it became real to me, that I was actually going to do it, everything we had—truly had, I believe it—became so clear to me, all the qualities that I loved and will miss. It's like I haven't just been grieving Melissa, I've been mourning you."

A choked sound escaped Cade and he resumed looking down, looking away.

"I'm grateful you're not a violent man, but some things do almost as much damage. I was losing myself, Cade. You didn't want me to work, so I didn't. You're not a super social guy, so we didn't entertain a lot. You and I both thought parents should be super invested in their children's lives, so we were—and I, as the stay-at-home-parent, especially was. I made Eva and Emily's activities, their wellbeing, their friendships and play dates my priority. And I never regretted it until . . . well, until I did."

Again Cade seemed about to speak, but again he let himself be shushed. "The problem with that way of living became especially clear when I didn't have Melissa anymore. That's when I realized what the cost was. That I had no one to turn to—none of my own close friends, no work to escape to for sanity—when you started up with . . . her and shut me out."

Cade went rigid beside her, but managed to refrain from contradicting.

"I was relieved when you finally seemed to get it, to understand that we should call it quits. And I don't know, maybe we still should. I love you, Cade. I wish I didn't sometimes, but I do. And just when I think I've managed to kill it off—or you finally have—you do something for me or for the kids, or look at me a certain way, or I'm stupid and let you touch me and then I'm back to where I started again. But love isn't enough if we keep making the same mistakes."

Noelle's hands ached from clenching them and she consciously paused, flexed her fingers, and took a deep breath. It was like a psychological cork had popped: all these things she'd had bottled up for months, for years, that she'd longed to say but held in lest she hurt Cade, lest they fight, lest he love her less, poured free. What, after all, was there to lose now? Nothing. And if there was anything to salvage or keep, this horrible way was the only possible path to doing it.

"I overheard you tell Callum you didn't actually cheat on me."

Cade inhaled like she'd stabbed him.

"But I know what I saw, so I don't know what you meant by your words. That you didn't stick your dick in her? I don't actually care. To me what you did was cheating. It baffles me—if you really feel you didn't cheat, why not clear it up with me? The only explanation I can come to is that maybe you weren't completely unfaithful, but you don't want to be with me anymore and you figure this is the easiest way to be done with me—I'll leave you and then you'll try to make me feel guilty in the hopes that I won't ask for as much support or something."

"You really think that little of me? Like if I can't have you, I would try to punish you?"

Noelle raised her hands palms up and shrugged. "I never would have thought so, but I feel like I hardly know you—or that maybe I was wrong about who I thought you were."

Cade responded with silence and Noelle knew they'd lost the battle. It took two people to fight for a relationship and apparently her husband was not that kind of man anymore, if he ever was.

Noelle sighed. "There's just one other thing I don't understand."

"Just one?" Usually that kind of comment would be a joke, but Cade's voice was quiet and serious.

"I'm so used to looking at you, trying to figure out what you're feeling or thinking, but unless we're having sex—and I don't trust anything we say or do in a moment of passion—your whole expression is totally closed off to me."

Cade cleared his throat. "Yeah?"

"Yeah. But the other night in the tent when the

girls were too scared to sleep alone . . . I caught you watching us and I was shocked."

Cade twisted to face her again and took one of her clenched fists in his hands. "Shocked how?"

Noelle didn't want to say the words, and for a second she thought she'd lose it. She bit her lip. "I . . . I thought for a moment I saw love, absolute love, in your eyes." Her voice broke. "How can you fake that? How?"

"God, Noelle." Cade rubbed her closed fist over his face and pressed his lips to her knuckles. "I wasn't faking it. I've never faked it. I do love you."

"So . . . please . . . just explain. Just . . . give me something, anything, to make this make sense." The back of Noelle's throat ached, but her eyes were dry. She had struggled to put how she honestly felt into words, and dammit, he was going to, too. He had to at least *try*. They'd shattered their life together, but they couldn't just throw out the pieces without at least trying to make sense of what happened.

A warm wind kicked up, pushing the branches of nearby trees into each other and lifting the duff on the trail, blowing it around. It sounded like even nature was whispering about them, making commentary on all their failings and weakness.

Just when Noelle was about to stand up, about to leave, sure that Cade wasn't going to speak, he did, his voice as quiet as the trees' and almost as hard to decipher.

"I . . . You . . ." He scrubbed his face with his palms and then looked over at her, the whites of his eyes gleaming in the moonlight, his expression desperate, almost wild. "You misunderstood . . . everything."

"So explain it to me, Cade."

He rubbed his face some more.

"I felt, I feel, exactly like you do. That I cheated on you. I stopped it, honestly, after some kissing, I swear—and I didn't even really want to kiss, I didn't look for it to happen, it was just"—his hands raked through his hair and he exhaled explosively—"*nothing.* It was nothing. I'd fallen asleep after a staff meeting where we'd all had some drinks—that's why I was such a mess. I'd loosened my tie, taken off my shoes, to sleep. I swear. And Sherry was, I don't know, feeling overly friendly or something."

Noelle tsked skeptically.

Cade closed his eyes, and his voice was so low it was almost a moan. "I know how it sounds. I know."

"So why not tell me all this then? Why not clear it up before it became this"—Noelle swept her hands through the air above her head—"this ginormous emotional shit show?"

"Because I wanted you to figure it out without me having to explain it to you. I wanted you to go back over our years together, to think about how I've always been with you and the girls and to know I wouldn't wreck it. I wanted you to love me and believe in me the way I believe in you."

Noelle jumped to her feet. "You're kidding, right? You wanted me to read your mind. *That's* your defense?"

Cade shrugged. "It's not much of one, I know. I figured that out when you and I had that fight over you having coffee with that guy."

"Oh, you did, hey? And just what was it that you figured out exactly?"

"That it didn't matter how well I thought I knew you ... I could still be terrified that you changed or that I'd been a fool. That maybe everything I was so proud of and sure of was a total crock. For the first time, instead of not understanding how you could instantly jump to that kind of suspicion about me, I saw it how you must've seen it, felt it ... and I realized it was true. I had been unfaithful—not sexually, whether you believe it or not, but by not respecting you enough to bring you into my circle, by not talking about it."

Noelle stood over him and tried to say something, but only managed a dry croaking sound. Cade reached for her hand again, but she moved away. He nodded as if that made sense.

"It's no defense for how stupid I was, how stupid I am—but I've just heard my dad's smooth bullshit my whole life. Words mean nothing and can say anything—or for some people anyway. I really thought that if I could keep being the guy I was before that night, you'd figure it out, you'd forgive me."

Noelle screwed her eyes shut, trying to stave off tears. What a complete and utter fool. And the craziest thing? She believed him, believed he had spent time thinking all this through and genuinely arrived at his insane conclusion, thinking it might work. Yet, for a guy who preferred to return the words "I love you" with a hug and a kiss, who was happy to not exchange more than a handful of words at a given time, he was doing quite the job of talking now. How much—and how long—had they each kept everything pent up inside and for what?

Noelle splayed her hands in front her, studying them so she didn't have to look at her husband. "I hear what you're saying, I do. And I even think I kind of understand where you were coming from—but I don't know if that's good enough. I thought you were done with me as a person, but wanted to keep a wife because it makes life so much easier for a man, or—"

Cade jammed his hands into his pockets and hunched his shoulders. "I've never just wanted 'a wife.' I only ever wanted you."

Noelle wrapped her arms around herself. "You have no idea how much I've wished that was true—and sometimes, in bed mostly, it even felt like it might be. More often though? It seems like a nanny or maid, cook, and chauffeur would mean just as much to you."

"Do we have to finish this conversation now?" Cade asked. "Hasn't it been a shitty enough night?"

Noelle nodded. "I actually meant to comfort you,

to see if you were all right, but everything just came up. And really, if not now, when?"

"Never. Never would've been good. If you could just know that you know me, we could go on like we were."

"Like we were?" Noelle shook her head. "That's what got us here. People change and grow, Cade—or they don't. And if they don't, they don't last. We didn't grow. We just got quieter and quieter and more resentful and more resentful. I'm afraid what was good between us is just memories of a distant thing, not something that still exists."

The wind died with Noelle's last comment and the surrounding forest went silent too, as if waiting to hear the final dregs of the conversation.

"So now what? Where do we go from here? Can we ever . . . can you . . . " Cade's voice, soft as rain on saturated ground, suddenly dried up.

Noelle pressed her head against his shoulder, and a crush of saltwater filled her sinuses, threatening to drown her.

"I don't know," she said miserably. "I just don't know."

Chapter 28

CADE TOOK NOELLE'S HAND ON the walk back to the main grounds and this time she didn't resist. The fact didn't lift his heart any. They were both quiet, but the mood between them wasn't tense or angry so much as it was heavy with thought. "Heavy with thought"—the figure of speech stuck in his craw. How useless thoughts were. Action was better. It accomplished stuff.

"Yeah," an inner voice sneered, sounding way too much like his father for his liking. "And how's that working out for you?"

Cade sighed and Noelle squeezed his hand just a little. This is it, Cade thought, the beginning of the end: polite and kind and killing me.

The parking area had emptied significantly and the dining and dance area, still glowing with tiny white lights, was also only sparsely populated now.

"Mommy! Daddy!" Emily had spotted them from wherever she'd been perched and came racing toward them. "Where were you?"

Eva followed wordlessly on her sister's heels. She

met Cade's eyes and her own were wide and solemn and filled with questions.

She knows, Cade thought. Noelle was right. Of course she knows. Like kids are ever spared their parents' unhappiness.

He dropped Noelle's hand, lifted Eva into a hug and tried to answer her unvoiced question. "Mom and I were just talking. Try not worry, okay? Everything's all right."

He put her down again. She didn't look any more convinced than he felt—but at least she spoke. "Are you, me and Em still going to be in the talent show tomorrow?"

"You guys are in the talent show? How come nobody told me?" Noelle asked, but for the time being was ignored.

Cade's brow furrowed. "Are you sure it's still on after—"

"It is!" Emily insisted and Eva nodded, backing her up. "Auntie Jo talked with everyone who's visiting from out of town and everyone asked if we can just finish the weekend off as planned."

Cade shrugged. "Well, I guess we better put the finishing touches on our performance then."

"But we still can't tell Mom or give her any hints, right?"

Eva groaned loudly. "You're so dumb! Now Mom knows it's about her."

"Don't worry," Noelle assured both girls. "I'll be

totally shocked. In fact, I've already forgotten all about it. Talent show, what talent show?"

"Phew, that was a close one," Emily whispered completely sincerely, making even Eva laugh.

"And are we still going fishing before it, like you promised?"

Noelle shot Cade a look. "First I've heard of it."

"Yeah, sorry. I was going to run it by you—just forgot," Cade said.

"It's okay," Noelle said. "I'll take a pass, though. Let you and the girls have some dad-daughter time."

Cade, much as he loved his kids, didn't want solo dad-daughter time right now, but he nodded anyway. "Let me just go confirm with Callum, and we'll head back to the campsite."

The girls were packed into the van when Cade returned, so he was a little surprised to find Noelle lingering outside the driver's door, waiting for him.

"I had another thought about our conversation earlier," she said. "And I'm sorry, but I didn't think it should wait."

"Okay, what?"

"Your silence about Sherry and so many other things over the years. It wasn't just about wanting me to know who you are without having to tell me, or about me believing in you, no matter what."

"Oh no?"

"No." Noelle shook her head. "It's also about your pride. Talking things out means accepting blame, or at least partial responsibility when or if things aren't perfect."

Cade grunted. Where was she going now?

"You're so afraid that admitting things aren't perfect—and that you aren't—is some huge failing or confirms your lunatic parents' poor opinion of you, that you'd rather let our relationship suffer. You'd rather save face than say we're struggling like every other human on the planet and risk looking weak or ordinary."

Cade grabbed the door handle, but paused before he opened it. "Wow, how insightful, Noelle." He actually meant it, so why he said it like such a jerk he wasn't sure. "But let's not pretend for one minute you don't like putting on a fake front and playing house like everything's perfect and nicey-nice just as much if not more than I do. You're so constantly worried about what other people think of you, of your looks, of your homemaking, of the house, of your parenting, that it's been years since you've considered anything in our relationship solely through our eyes—the only people whose opinions should matter one flying fuck."

Noelle inhaled sharply, turned on her heel, and stormed to her side of the vehicle.

Then, of all the things Cade had endured that night, Noelle mumbled what might have been the most confusing of all.

"Well, at least we're finally getting somewhere."

Noelle slept in Eva's tent that night and the girls

gave sleeping sans parents one more shot, bundled up together in Emily's tent. Cade didn't hear a thing from any of the key people in his life, and as he lay listening to the night sounds of the forest around him, he wondered if this evening was a harbinger what was to come: each of them going it alone and apart in a familiar and growing darkness.

Chapter 29

TRUE TO HER WORD—NOT THAT Cade had held out much hope of otherwise—Noelle did not go fishing with them, despite the girls' begging and cajoling.

"I haven't had much alone time," she said. "I'm going for a quick swim, then I want to shower so I'm ready for the day. And then, if it's okay with Callum, I'll borrow his car and go into town. I want to sit in a coffee shop, listen to the hum of civilization, and smell something besides pine trees."

"Why?" Emily was genuinely confused, but Cade thought he got it. Their time up north was rapidly coming to an end and he suspected Noelle was going to miss it, or some aspects of it at least, as much as he was. She'd been outside digging in the dirt, trekking down trails, and soaking up the great outdoors almost as much as the kids. She was trying to prepare herself for their return to city life.

Callum, shitty as ever at reading Cade's not-subtle-at-all body language, agreed to lend his car—and that simply, that easily, she was free of him.

Noelle crawled out of the tent in that new bathing

suit of hers just as he, Callum and the girls were about to head down to the dock. Something gleamed in her hand.

She made her way to Callum, holding out her palm, revealing the shining metal bits of a fishing lure.

As she told the story of how she'd found it, the girls were delighted and a bit nervous.

"They won't swoop down on us while we're fishing, will they?" Emily asked.

"I love crows," Eva said wistfully. "But they're kind of scary too."

Callum took the lure from Noelle and nodded at his nieces. "I know what you mean, but I think lots of things in life are like that. Wonderful, but scary. You just have to be brave like your mom. Who knows, maybe that's the secret to finding treasures."

"Mom's not brave," Eva scorned.

"I don't know. She wrangles two monsters every day, seems brave to me."

"Two monsters?" Emily asked.

Callum grinned. "Well, three, if you count your dad."

"What—hey!" Eva exclaimed with mock outrage. "Mom, Uncle Callum just called us monsters."

Noelle smiled. "Well, if the shoe fits."

"Yeah, if the monster shoe fits!" Emily broke into giggles. Eva rolled her eyes.

"Are they still good?" Noelle asked, bobbing her chin toward the small gold and silver spoon shapes glinting in Callum's hand.

He nodded. "I'm sure they are. They just need to be tied back together, and held in place with something. Jo swears by a wedding band."

Cade reached out and took the lure from his brother. "I'll try it. It's been years since I fished. Maybe they'll bring me luck."

"And it'll kind of be like Mom's with us, too," Emily said.

Cade tousled Emily's hair, but caught Noelle's gaze. "Well, sort of maybe, but nowhere near as good as if she really was."

Noelle looked away.

IN FRONT OF THEM, UNCUT by his and Callum's canoe, the smooth-as-glass lake reflected the sky and looked robin egg blue. Cade glanced back at the girls in their red canoe, laughing and paddling. They were more interested in practicing how to turn than in baiting a hook and putting a line in.

"Okay, you're right," Cade admitted. "They are ready to handle the boat on their own."

"Wait, I'm sorry, can you repeat that? I thought you said I was right about something."

"Yeah, yeah. Don't get too excited. Once in a lifetime and miracles and all that."

Callum laughed and handed him a rod. "Anyway, don't worry about it. I get it. They're your kids. It's better to be safe than sorry, right? Over protective than not protective enough?"

"Yeah, but I have to remember there's a balance. They need to push themselves, do challenging things, maybe even scary things, and discover it's okay if they fail or fall on their faces, or they'll never learn to take risks or discover the difference between safe and foolish chances."

Cade cast his line with a whirring-zip, and he was surprised by the pleasure that welled up deep inside him as he watched his lure drop in a perfect arc. He wasn't someone who felt young very often, but out there, surrounded by the sweet lake air, the girls' bubbling laughter, and the occasional buzz of a shimmering green or purple dragonfly, he felt like the boy he'd been so long ago—except happy.

"Nice cast, bro."

"Thanks."

"What, no brag?"

Cade just shrugged.

Small waves lapped against the side of the canoe and it rocked gently. Cade enjoyed the moment, mercifully free of thoughts of Noelle. Then Callum spoke and shattered Cade's brief sanctuary.

"So what are you going to do?"

Cade didn't bother to pretend he didn't know what Callum was talking about. What was the point? Callum already knew he was screwed. Everyone did. He shot a look behind him. The girls were nearby, focused on their rods now. Cade was conscious of how well voices carried over water, but still . . . it might be good to run his thoughts past someone, and since his little brother had somehow ended up happily married, he was probably his best bet. He lowered his voice and shared the past few days as factually as he could.

"Yeah, Mom and Dad, hey? I don't even know how to go there," was the only interruption Callum made, inserted when Cade mentioned leaving the dinner party after Caren's announcement.

"I just couldn't take it . . . I don't know. It seems like an omen of what's in store for me, no matter what I do."

Callum shook his head and moved his hand almost like he was taking invisible notes as Cade voiced, despite his huge embarrassment, his thoughts when he and Noelle shared the tent, the big fight they'd had, and her cryptic words.

When he finished, Callum was quiet and they both reeled in. It wasn't until Callum cast again that he spoke. "It seems like, maybe, you're in a good place."

Cade let out a barking laugh. What the hell had he expected? Gold advice?

"No, seriously. Noelle was right. At least you guys are arguing—and about your real issues, not just secondary crap."

"Oh yeah, it's fantastic. Now we can really rip the shit out of each other and cause some real wounds before we split." He remembered the girls and looked back again. They were drifting about twenty feet away, but Eva's eyes, so like Noelle's, met his and he knew she'd heard. Shit. But again, not like he and Noelle really had any secrets from them.

"Hey, girls, row closer, okay? You're getting too far away."

Eva looked surprised, probably expecting to be told to stop listening or to be ignored. She and Emily did as bidden though, reeled in and took up their paddles.

"So, what . . . you're just giving up?"

"No." The girls splashed closer. "No, of course not. But I don't know what to do."

"Yes, you do, Daddy. Remember the talent show?" Emily called.

Cade shut his eyes. Yes, he remembered the talent show—and what he'd, in an idiotically optimistic fit, suggested to the girls.

"Tell Uncle Callum, Dad," Eva said seriously, as if reading his mind, knowing his insecurities. "See what he thinks."

Again, Callum listened without jest or criticism. When Cade was done, Emily was bouncing excitedly in her seat and Eva was nagging, "Don't, *don't*. You'll make us tip."

"Settle down, honey," Cade agreed.

Emily stilled a little. "But it's going to be so fun. Mommy will love it, Daddy—she will. And then you guys can be happy again and me and Eva can be happy again, too."

Cade wondered if broken hearts actually bled. It

232

felt like it. What had he done to his kids? Set them up for further pain and bigger questions?

Callum was nodding thoughtfully, however. "I think it's a good idea."

"You do?" Doubt furrowed Cade's brow.

"Yeah, I mean, she thinks your pride will always get in the way of your relationship, right?"

Cade nodded.

"And that you care more about how things between you look than how they actually are . . . Well, if you do this, it'll show her that's not true because you'll pretty much shoot your pride all to hell."

Cade cracked his knuckles. "Gee thanks, buddy. Thanks a ton."

Callum shrugged and gave a small grin, but his eyes were squinty and sympathetic.

Chapter 30

NOELLE HAD COME UP WITH the idea on her way into town and she smiled at her and the girls' handiwork. The big vase of roses and glitter-encrusted, star-topped sticks they'd made looked great. She set them on the platform beside the mic. Each performer would receive one of the star sticks as a souvenir, and Emily was beside herself with anticipation. Even Eva thought they were "cool."

A small crowd had already assembled in front of the temporary stage, constructed from risers Jo had borrowed from some church, complete with a rented sound system and a backdrop of white lights salvaged from the dinner party. *The dinner party*. Ugh. Noelle winced whenever she thought of it, though somehow, bizarrely, it hadn't seemed to dampen anyone's enthusiasm much. Brian was as flirty and silly as ever—though Noelle noted the girl on his arm was a waif-thin brunette now, the redhead from just two weeks ago already replaced. Callum was keeping busy. Cade was . . . hard to read.

He and the girls were already back at River's Sigh

when Noelle arrived earlier, craft goodies in tow, and he'd herded the girls her way after "practicing" whatever surprise they had planned for the talent show. She wondered what the kids had up their sleeves and what role Cade would play in the whole thing. They'd left Eva's flute at home and Jo didn't have a piano. Maybe they'd worked out a gymnastics routine and Cade was their spotter?

She tapped the mic and said test, test just to make Emily cheer. It worked and she grinned at her daughter's excitement, then headed back to the kitchen to see if Jo needed help with any last minute things.

"Everything's good to go," she said, entering the fragrant room. Jo turned from the platter of desserts she was arranging.

"And does it look like people are going to show up?"

"It does indeed." Noelle fetched a spatula and started lifting tiny spanakopita triangles onto a plate Jo had waiting beside other appetizers. "It's kind of bizarre actually. I think pretty much everyone came out—though no Caren or Duncan, of course."

"Bizarre is right." Jo shook her head and hefted the largest platter of food. "Though I don't know why anything surrounding Duncan or Caren surprises me anymore."

Noelle followed her out the swinging door, carrying two trays. She caught up to Jo at the big tables beside the almost full rows of chairs. Everyone was chatting merrily and Noelle wasn't overly concerned with being overheard. "Do you think . . . well, is Callum all right?"

Jo settled her dish amidst the others she'd already put out. "I think he was shocked by the timing—and that it might happen for real—but he isn't unhappy about it. Cade?"

Noelle shrugged and waited for Jo to be ready for another plate of food, since she seemed to have a system for how she wanted it laid out. "He's sad. Thinks it's an omen or some crazy thing about how we'll end up. He seems . . . resigned. I don't think he'll resist us getting divorced."

Jo paused, studied Noelle's face, then took the last plate of goodies from Noelle. "I see. And is that what you really want?"

Noelle didn't get a chance to answer. Emily showed up at her elbow and tugged her away with an earnest, "Mom, Mom, Mom."

"Okay, I'm coming. What?"

Emily pushed a folded envelope into her hand. It was beaten up and the crease practically had holes. "Daddy said, if you wouldn't mind, he'd like you to read this before the show."

"What is it?"

"No clue." Emily skipped away like she didn't have a care in the world—which was totally untrue, of course, but Noelle was beyond grateful for the way childhood let you dip in and out of sorrow, giving you a break from your worries. She and Cade still had a chance to figure out what to do, how to act in the best way as to not permanently scar the kids—but time was critical now. They either had to heal or make a clean break. They couldn't keep festering or the infection would slowly do lasting damage to everyone. She already saw differences in Eva, noticed how she watched them warily, seemed too attentive to their squabbles, and was extra animated—like she was desperate almost—when they weren't fighting.

She smoothed the envelope in her hand, then opened it. Jo breezed by on yet another mission, patting her shoulder on her way past. "Ten minutes 'til go time."

Noelle flashed two thumbs up and was rewarded by Jo's grin. She turned her attention back to the letter. White paper, nothing fancy, and Cade's simple, straightforward printing across the page.

Dear Noelle,

If you're reading this, it means I've lost everything and we're probably done because I'm an idiot. I wanted to spare myself—and you—my pathetic begging, but I think I've always known sometime, somewhere, it would come to this, so I'm writing this now and plan to carry it on me wherever I go. Maybe it will be a good luck charm. (Does that idea make you smile even a little bit? Does anything I do or say ever make you smile anymore? I hope so because all I

*want to do is make you smile and be the rea-
son you smile for the rest of our lives.)*

*Whether it works as a charm or not, I do
hope it will prevent the break up of our marriage by reminding me constantly of what I
want—you and the girls and the home we built
together—not that I need reminded of that. I
never forget that. What I forget is to act in a
way that gives me an ice cube's chance in hell
of getting what I want: to keep you.*

*I'm not good at saying things out loud, but
I think them and so I'm going to write some of
them out. Please read them and try to hear
them how I mean them. I love you and the
girls. Deeply. Fully. Totally. I can't imagine ever
being with anyone but you and I don't want to.
I did not sleep with, did not have sex, with
that other woman OR WITH ANY OTHER
WOMAN, but you are right. I was unfaithful to
you, the actual mechanics of my actions aren't
important. Just by being there with her like
that betrayed you and my vows. And worse. I
know I shut you out—the thing you've always
hated most (or so you say—though by now I've
given you such a list of things to hate, maybe I
have other more hated qualities in your eyes),
but I just felt so . . . ashamed. Especially considering the timing. You needed me more than*

ever in the hard year after Melissa died and I let you down in a way that . . . almost makes me unable to breath.

I wanted you to decide on your own, without me having to prove it, that I would, of course, come to my senses and do the honorable thing. I wanted you to know me. To love me no matter what.

Here the letter was interrupted and in a slightly different shade of blue ink there was a scrawled arrow to a sentence that read, *Why the hell did I think it was on you to read my mind or decide anything about my intentions without me giving full disclosure I will never know. Also I do get that you can't know me if I don't let you in.*

Hurt and confusion pulsed through Noelle in time to her heartbeat. She read on.

Even harder, I know that we wouldn't be where we are, on the edge of not being together, if this misunderstanding about Sherry was our only issue. The ball is in your court. I don't want a divorce. I want to fight and keep you—keep us. I will go to counseling (and stick a fork in my eye—same thing, right? Please laugh at that, even just a little), or do whatever you want, whatever it takes . . . but I also don't want to keep hurting you or the girls. In your heart of hearts, if you're done with me, let me know. If you choose me, I will spend the rest of our days grateful for this second chance. If you can't forgive me, I do understand—after all, I can't forgive myself—and I just want you to know I will always love you and do my best to provide for you and our beautiful daughters forever.

Sincerely,
Cade

There was one p.s.—again written in the slightly different blue ink.

I don't know how I didn't get it, didn't see this through your eyes, how it would've felt, how it had to have felt. What I hate most is how my actions—or inaction, lack of communication—changed how you saw yourself. I was angry because I thought the Sherry thing unfairly colored your opinion of me. Over the past few weeks—watching you get ready to leave me and returning to your true self in the way you dress, take charge, and have fun—I've been heartbroken because I see so clearly how my actions changed how you felt about yourself and I can only say I'm sorry . . . which is a totally bogus, useless word, however much I mean it. Feel it. I am sorry.

Noelle's throat was on fire. That bastard. That manipulative, selfish, rotten bastard. How could he give this to her now of all times? How dare he? But then again, they were so close to the brink, maybe she did understand his timing. Maybe he thought it was his last chance, *their* last chance. And maybe it was.

She closed her eyes, swallowing hard. She couldn't fall apart until the night was over. Hold it together, she commanded herself. *Hold it together.*

Somehow Noelle did manage to keep a grip on her scattered emotions. In fact, by some miracle, she even managed to be distracted by the performances, laughing out loud at some of them and being honestly blown away by others—though she shouldn't have been. It never failed to amaze her: as messed up as Cade's family was, there was no denying the talent and intellect that seemed to run through their gene pool just as strongly as the dysfunction.

And people loved the star sticks they got for participating. Every time Noelle handed one out, Emily made an okay sign with her thumb and finger and bounced up and down in the front row where she sat with cousins from Caren's side, eyes shining. Eva was glowing and laughed brightly more than once. Noelle's heart panged a little. It was so good to see her serious eldest enjoying herself.

There'd been eleven performances in all, plus an intermission, and the buffet tables of snack food were seriously depleted when Noelle's finger traced a line to the final performers—her very own . . . Cade. She read the line again, mentally kicking herself for not reading through the whole list earlier to prepare for what might be coming—but then again, she'd been preoccupied. The contents of Cade's letter skittered back into her mind and her mouth went cotton dry.

"And now," she croaked, then cleared her throat, took a sip of water and tried again. "Last but not least, the . . . Cade."

"*The Cade*—catchy group name," Brian quipped from the audience, causing a wave of laughter.

Cade bounded onto the stage in beat up jeans, a tight white tank top, and, of all things, a black cowboy hat. Dammit if Noelle's heart—or her hormones anyway—didn't jump a little. He held out one of his well-muscled, tanned arms in a sweeping, welcoming gesture and grabbed the mic with his free hand. "Let's put it together for my back up babes, Eva and Emily."

More laughter rippled at the line "back up babes," and there was a roar of clapping and stomping feet as the babes themselves rocketed onto the stage.

Noelle could only shake her head. What were they planning—and where had the kids gotten sequined body suits, pink flared skirts, cowboy boots and white Stetsons?

"Now you all know me," Cade crooned into the mic. "And you know I'm not a singer."

"It's true," Emily squeaked, lifting on tiptoes to put her mouth near the mic. "He's really not."

The crowd belly-laughed at that, then laughed even harder when Eva rolled her eyes, showing that her sister had gone off script.

"But a cowboy can change his boots and learn a new tune," Cade added, still speaking in a silly mock cowboy twang.

"And hoo-whee, boy, you'd better change those boots," Brian hollered. "Your feet stink."

In response, Cade did some two-step jig thing that Noelle didn't even know he knew how to do. The girls swayed back and forth like the Supremes.

The crowd responded appreciatively yet again, and Noelle tried not to think about the letter or the surreal quality of the moment. Just let me enjoy my family for whatever it is, whatever we have, right now, she prayed.

Cade stepped forward, mic still in hand, but his voice fell back to its normal deep tenor and went somber. "I do have to apologize in advance to Lonestar for how I'm about to butcher their great song, 'Let's Be Us Again,' but I just want to say I'm so grateful they wrote it because it says a lot of things I've never been brave enough to say."

There was a collective inhale from the crowd, and Cade pushed on. "I mean every word and I couldn't let another night go by without publicly expressing my regrets for the kind of husband I've been—and haven't been—to my wife. This song's for you, hon."

His eyes found Noelle's and held them. A tight

band of longing and sorrow squeezed around her chest. Then he looked at their two daughters and grinned. When they popped their thumbs up, he nodded at Callum who sat right stage, handling the sound.

In all truth, he was probably terrible, but Noelle would've had no way of telling. She felt seared, like the words Cade sang, a little rough, maybe slightly off tune, but so surprisingly sweetly were branded into her. *Let's be us again.* The refrain played through her again and again. Was it really so simple as that, she wondered. Just deciding to be themselves again, working it through, giving it another try?

The audience was still cheering crazily and clapping like mad as Noelle made her way back to the podium. She took the mic from Cade, trembling slightly, hardly able to look at him. Emily and Eva each took one of their father's hands and bowed and bowed.

"Well, well, well," she boomed, shocking herself at how smooth and unflustered she sounded. "That was the . . . Cade."

The audience roared at the repeat of her earlier fumble, the tiny inside joke. They really were easy to please. She turned slightly, facing the stage, facing her family. "That was . . . beautiful, guys. Just beautiful. Sincerely." Her voice caught as she echoed Cade's sign off from the letter—and then Aisha was suddenly there, rescuing her.

"We have one more impromptu performance," she

said. "I call it 'Mo plays a mean pot lid.'" A jangling children's song piped through the speakers. The crowd turned their attention to baby Mo dressed up as a tiger. Noelle fled.

Chapter 31

CADE FOUND NOELLE IN THE same place she'd found him after yesterday's dinner party fiasco. Hopefully public Archer-marriage-issue performances weren't going to become a new thing. It was earlier and not as dark as last night had been, however, and he had no problem spotting her on the deck, huddled against one of the wide cedar beams that framed the door, arms wrapped around her knees. She looked like a kid. And maybe that was fitting. Maybe in some ways everyone was still a kid, inexperienced, terrified by whatever new injury or surprise life hurled at them.

He climbed the stairs slowly. He was beat. Dead beat. So tired he was shocked he could even lift his limbs. He sank down beside his wife—ex-wife?—put an arm around her and pulled her close, then buried his face in the sweet cloud of her hair. He breathed deeply, wanting to commit every nuance of her scent and the soft weight of her in his arms to memory.

"I'm sorry," he whispered. "I thought . . . I thought it was a good idea. And then, well, it was too late."

She cricked her neck and looked up at him. She

had rubbed her make-up into Alice Cooper worthy black circles beneath her eyes. She didn't say anything.

He bit his lip and nodded—then confusion mingled with his grief and dread. She was . . . smiling and her eyes were soft. Raccoon-eyed or not, she had never been more beautiful to him.

"I do forgive you," she whispered. "If you can forgive me."

His breath hitched so hard it hurt his chest. "You mean it?"

She nodded, but he needed to hear it out loud.

"Yeah, I mean it, but only if you swear you meant those things you said, that you really want me, will honor *me*." She pressed her hands to the sides of his face and met his eyes with such a wide open, hide-nothing gaze that he wondered if they'd ever truly seen each other before this close call, this terrible near-tragedy of almost losing each other.

"I don't want to live without you anymore than you want to live without me," she continued. "And I don't want to share custody or go through the agony of splitting up our family, dividing our home, wrecking the life we've built." She took a wavering breath. "But I won't stand for it again. I can't. I don't care if you didn't sleep with her. It was enough. It was too much. You hurt me so much. I never used to doubt you, doubt us—and now I look in the mirror and I only see flaws. I hear my voice and I don't recognize the unhappy, nagging shrew I've become. I don't know if I'm enough for you—"

He cut her off, vehemently, numb and thick-tongued with remorse. "No. No. That's the worst thing—like I said in my letter—that my stupid ego made you insecure. It was never about you not being enough. It was always about me, being a jerk, being weak, being afraid."

"What has happened has happened, we can't go back—but we also can't lose our way like this again. We have to do better. If there's a second time, there is no second—"

"I agree."

"And . . ." She took a deep breath. "I'm going back to work, something part-time maybe. I still want lots of time with you and the girls, but I need . . . independence. And I'm doing my own yard work again. I don't give a shit if I never have another manicure."

Cade caught her hand and gently bit her thumb. "Whatever you want, whatever you need. I love knowing you're at home, taking care of things, taking care of us—but I'll love knowing you're happy and taking care of you and showing the girls how to take care of themselves properly even more."

"Really? Are you sure because—"

"Shhh." He leaned in and kissed her mouth.

She pulled back. "Cade . . ." A tinge of alarm lifted the volume of her voice.

"Don't worry," he said, kissing her again. "We will talk and talk and talk some more, as much as you need, whenever you need, on our own, with a shrink—I'll even do couples' therapy, like I promised, God forbid."

She laughed a little at that and the fear in Cade's chest—that this was all a ruse, a misunderstanding on his part because he wanted it so badly—eased.

He completed his thought against the soft flesh at the base of her throat and his breath on her skin made her shiver. "But for right now, wife . . . just let me kiss you."

And Noelle did.

Chapter 32

"IT'S A GOOD THING AISHA remembered to give me and Eva our star sticks after our song tonight, isn't it?" Emily asked for the millionth time.

"It sure is," Noelle assured her, then snuggled her into her bed at Chinook cabin. Jo had insisted they forgo the campground and resume staying at River's Sigh immediately. "I have no idea what happened to Rick. He just never showed—but Duncan says he's fine, for whatever that's worth. The place is ready and waiting for you. And the camping gear will be fine. The gate's locked until tomorrow. Callum and Cade can grab things in the morning." She'd given Noelle a searching look too, asking with her eyes how things with Cade had gone. Noelle thought her smile was polite but private. Jo, however, got a look of glee, nodded happily and bounced away as energetically as Emily might have.

Later, once Eva was tucked in too, Noelle and Cade sat on the couch in the big living room. "The worst of the heat seems to be over with," he said, rubbing his arms. "We might even get to use that thing before we leave." He gestured at the empty stone fireplace across from where they cuddled. "Mmhm," she said, drowsily.

"You sound exhausted. Let me take you to bed."

She laughed. "Soon, soon. I just want to . . . enjoy this for a bit first."

He bent his head and kissed her shoulder. She could feel his smile against her skin.

"I was thinking," he said a moment later.

"Did it hurt?" she quipped, exactly the way she always used to.

"Har har," he whispered—and really, his breath on her flesh was the hottest thing. "I'm serious. Jo never did manage to get ahold of the Justice of the Peace— and he doesn't have an answering machine."

Noelle straightened in her seat. "So?"

"So," he said, nuzzling her neck. "I was thinking . . . maybe we should stand in at the renewal of vows."

"What? You mean like instead of your parents?"

"Well, unless something drastic has changed, they won't be using the services they paid for. Whaddya say?"

Noelle imagined a bouquet of the fuchsia roses she'd helped resurrect—so pretty and symbolic. And she could wear the gauzy sundress she'd purchased—

She shook her head abruptly. "I think . . . well, let's just keep our relationship between us and with the girls. It doesn't matter what people say or think. I want us to be solid in our own hearts and minds. That's all I need."

Cade's face held such fondness that she suddenly felt weepy. "Sounds good to me—better than good. Even as I asked, I was wondering what was wrong with me. I must've left my balls at the campsite."

Noelle laughed, then looked down pointedly and arched an eyebrow. "Oh, really? That's unfortunate because I'd been thinking—"

Cade growled. "No worries. It was just a joke to get you to feel sorry for me."

"Are you trying to get in my pants?"

"Always. Would it work?"

"Like a charm."

Chapter 33

NOELLE STUDIED THE WHITE COTTON panty liner fixed to her underwear and bit her lip. Not a trace of pink, no matter how she hoped differently. Her period should've arrived two or three days ago and she was never late. They'd used condoms the past few nights, so that only left . . . the therapy night. Dammit.

It wasn't that another baby would be bad, but it wasn't exactly great timing either. Yes, she and Cade were back on track, but she wasn't going to fall prey to a false sense of "Oh, we're okay now" and just leave off working through their issues like she'd done in the past. They needed to learn how to really talk—not incessantly, but honestly. Noelle didn't mind a strong, silent type. She didn't require, or want, Cade to provide every need, and she was going to make women friends again, but she also didn't want him bottling up God knows what and letting it poison everything—and that advice applied to her, too. She was going to, as she was always coaching the girls to do, find her words, *use* her words.

So she didn't know what to pray. Praying against a

baby seemed wrong—but it would complicate things that were already complicated.

She was just about to head down Chinook's big staircase to see what the girls were up to when a happy Cade bounded up the stairs and into the bedroom. "My mom just showed up. I think she's doing all right. She's taking the kids into town for lunch." His smile faded when he saw Noelle's face.

"What's wrong?"

It was on the tip of her tongue to say, "Nothing."

But—and it made her heart skip to let her mind rest on the thought—she was optimistic about this new start of theirs. She didn't want to wreck it by reverting to her old, button everything up and tuck it away self. If she was worried, she should let Cade be worried too. Sharing how you were feeling wasn't the same thing as nagging or stressing someone else out. She hoped.

"I'm late."

It took a second for him to understand what she was saying, but when he did, nothing could've prepared her for his response.

He swooped her into the air, holding her close, and spun her around. "A baby? You're sure? See, I still have it!"

What was it with this man and his extreme pride in his ability to knock her up? She felt herself grin like a mad woman. "Oh, yes, you're incredibly virile."

He set her down, matched her grin, and pretended to beat his chest, which made her laugh out loud. Then his expression changed and he searched her face. "How are you with all this? I should've asked that first. Is it a happy surprise?"

"Well, right now I'm a little stunned—but it's, *I'm*, happy, I think. It's early days though, and like I said it's just that I'm late. I haven't done a test. It might not be anything at all. I only told you so you'd know what was on my mind, so you wouldn't worry."

"But you're usually like a clock, right?"

"Yeah."

"Okay, well, I'll hold off buying booties, but I'll pick up pickles and ice cream."

Noelle shook her head. "Good plan." A moment later she added, "And if I'm not pregnant, if it is just a false alarm, will you be very disappointed?"

Cade hesitated for a fraction of a second and Noelle's stomach tugged. He would be. And he wasn't going to be honest about it, wanting to spare her feelings—or avoid his own or some such nonsense. How easily they fell back into old, bad patterns—

"Yes, I think I will be, which is weird because I always thought we'd had our two and that was the plan, so that was it. I always felt done. But I'm good either way. Seriously."

Love and appreciation for Cade rolled over her, as heady and all encompassing as any of the passion of their early days. And in its wake trickled a deep awareness and affirmation that she hadn't even known she needed: She loved Cade Archer. Still. Deeply.

They had almost let it die, cutting off all the blooms, pruning away any new growth—but the roots had remained. Dormant. Waiting. Thank God Cade had pushed for this trip. She shuddered to think what may have happened to them, the disastrous choice she might have made.

Oh, she wasn't so silly as to think she'd never love again. She probably would. People just did—if they'd stop fighting it anyway. But she'd never love the way she loved Cade. There was something incredibly poignant about first loves—and how lucky were they? They'd married their first true loves.

Only loves, something inside her whispered.

Something her mom said years earlier that hadn't made sense at the time came back to Noelle: "It's not the raging anger at your husband you have to be wary of. It's indifference." Thank goodness they'd had this breakthrough while they still felt passionate toward each other, not completely deadened.

She wasn't aware of her tears until Cade spoke in a low, concerned voice. "What's wrong? Are you all right?"

He was standing very, very close, his broad chest just inches from her. He put his arm loosely around her and his big hand edged beneath the gauzy hem of her sleeveless blouse. The heat of his palm against her lower back sent a shuddering tremor of want through her. The core of her actually ached with it.

She stared up at him and his eyes burned with the

desire she felt. "I'm great."

She removed his hand though, and disappointment showed in his face. She reached up and rubbed his stubbled jaw. His eyes blazed brighter again at her touch.

"I like this new look," she said.

"Oh, yeah?" he whispered back.

"Yeah." Her voice was a croak, not the sexiest thing, perhaps, although you'd never know it from the fever in his eyes and the hardness of him against her stomach.

He'd stepped closer, as if accepting that she'd moved his hand, but challenging the notion she'd get rid of him so quickly. If only he knew. She wasn't planning on putting him off. Anything but. Another current sparked between them, so hot she was practically surprised to not see a white bolt of energy light the air.

She stepped back and he gave her a disbelieving look, like he'd felt the zap too and couldn't understand why they weren't already doing something about it.

"It's the middle of the afternoon," she said.

Cade sighed and shifted awkwardly, unable to hide his obvious desire. His eyes continued to burn into hers, challenging her.

She bit her lip, gave him a wink, and sank down onto the amazing bed they'd been blessed to share, and realized their bed at home was getting a downgrade that would really be a huge upgrade. She wanted a denim quilt and crisp cotton sheets, something tough and durable—that they could mess the hell up and would only become softer and more beautiful with wear.

"I'm sweaty and gross," she whispered apologetically, letting her legs fall open. Her long airy skirt fluttered like a kiss against her calves. "And I haven't shaved since—" Her words drifted off, the ending clear to both of them . . . *since the last time we did this.*

Cade gave her a lecherous look, trailing his gaze over her chest, along her torso, down her legs—then back up. "And I love *that*," he growled.

Noelle laughed, buzzing with pure joy. "Well, good grief, man, then get down to business already— wait, where are the kids again?"

"With my mom." Cade's face broke into his triumphant Viking god grin. Heat surged through her. How good it was to see him smile so often again. "Now, that's what I'm talking about," he added and very obediently got down to business as commanded. In the middle of the day. With the lights on and the show-everything sun pouring through the windows.

Their last days at River's Sigh passed too quickly—and, typical, Noelle's period arrived just in time for a long road trip. Awesome. She was a bit ashamed by the relief that coursed through her.

"Too bad," Cade said when she told him. "Should we, do you want to, try again, maybe?"

She reached out and stroked his cheek. "I don't

think so. Let's wait a bit. See where we are in a year or two, then take it from there."

Cade searched her eyes, then crossed the room in big strides. Their bags were stacked by the bedroom door, ready to load into the van. For a minute she wondered if he was going to kick them or find some other way to explosively avoid whatever feelings were tumbling through him. She needn't have worried. He took a deep breath. "That makes good sense. You're right—but your words hurt a little—no, they terrify me. I'm in for the long haul. I want a fifteenth anniversary with you. And a thirtieth. I want a friggen Silver Jubilee for crying out loud. I know I haven't earned that, but—"

She stopped him there, pressing a finger to his lips to stem his sweet rush of insecurity. "No, no. You misunderstood. I want all that too. Have always wanted that—with you. I just meant . . ." She broke off, suddenly shy, then pushed on. "Eva and Emily are at such a wonderful, fun age—and they no longer demand every minute of our care or attention. I kind of like being able to sneak away to just . . . enjoy each other."

"Oh," said Cade.

Noelle smiled up at him.

"*Oh*," he said again, and now he was smiling too. "God, you're insatiable, woman."

Noelle grinned smugly. "Yep, get used to it."

"I can probably manage," Cade said with a long-suffering sigh. Noelle smacked him.

"It's not just the sex, you know," she added a moment later.

Cade put down the bag he'd just lifted and crossed the room to her. "I do know." He pressed his lips to hers and Noelle wondered if she'd ever had a sweeter kiss. "It's that you are flesh of my flesh, blood of my blood. My other half. The better part."

She wondered what other things this now-talking-up-a-storm husband of hers kept stored in his head. "That's exactly how I feel," she agreed. "But I wouldn't have been able to say it half so eloquently."

Cade broke their embrace, headed to the big picture window, and searched for something. Then he nodded and turned back. "The kids are happily throwing sticks for the mutts. Would you care to give the master bedroom a formal good-bye?"

Noelle scrunched her nose. "Well, I don't know. . . . It's the middle of the morning, check out time's right around the corner, and we have a ten hour drive ahead of us before we stop for the night—"

Cade growled. "I'll take that as a yes, absolutely, I'm dying for you, husband."

She shrieked with laughter as he scooped her up, then said, "I'm serious, Cade. Not right now."

He set her down, looking quizzical.

"It's not that I don't want to—or that I don't love this place. I'd like to visit here every year from now on. It's just that I'm ready, past ready, to get back to our house, our bed, our *home*."

Cade's eyes creased and he nodded. "So what are we standing around talking for?"

Epilogue

BACK AT HOME, THE KIDS settled in and got caught up with their new school year. Cade went back to work, and Noelle happily sought a new groove. She had two job applications out and a whole flowerbed of bulbs planted. Fall had come, but their weeks at River's Sigh weren't forgotten. Low afternoon rays glinted prettily off the sun catcher Noelle and the girls had made as a memento. Eva was partial to its bright shards of colored glass. Emily's favorite part was the driftwood she'd collected from the creek at River's Sigh B & B. But Noelle? Noelle loved the gold and silver spoons from the old fishing lure she'd reclaimed when they'd been packing to leave. They reminded her of their holidays, yes, but also made her, weirdly perhaps, think of her and Cade.

The phone rang and Cade answered it, his voice a cozy rumble from his chair—until he suddenly yelled, "Are you kidding me? *No*. No way."

Eva, Emily and Noelle looked up from where they were sitting around the coffee table, picking activities for the year. Noelle had limited them to one extracurricular activity per semester plus music lessons for one instrument. "We need time to visit and just hang out as a family—and you guys need time to just play," she'd said when the girls seemed shocked. Neither of them objected at all and Noelle wished she'd figured this out a few years earlier. Ah, well. Live and learn, right?

Cade lowered his voice, but still sounded adamant. "No," he repeated. "I've already told you, Callum. No dogs. It's Noelle's rule. She's always been firm on it. No—no, don't put Jo on."

Cade didn't get a word in edgewise for several seconds and his expression grew pained. Finally he sighed in defeat and glanced over at Noelle. "It's Jo. I guess that monster mutt of Dave's needs a new home. He's going traveling or something—but wants a permanent family for the dog. He approached Callum of all things and for some reason he and Jo think you'd want him."

"Destroy-a-con?" Noelle said. "Really?"

"Or, Henry. I bet if we renamed him Henry he'd be much better behaved," Emily said.

"We'd definitely play outside more—and we'd be safer—if we had a large dog," Eva added.

Cade slapped his forehead. "I can't believe this. Let me call you back, Jo." He ended the call and looked at Noelle in bewilderment. "You're honestly considering this?"

Noelle stood up, crossed over to him, and gave him a hug. "Maybe. I think so. He's a terrible dog, after all.

Big and badly behaved. I think he'll be hard to find a home for."

"You're really selling me on him, honey."

Noelle laughed.

Emily made a high-pitched excited noise, then clamped down on it immediately as if not wanting to jinx her chances. She bounced on the couch.

"And he and I have an understanding," Noelle said.

"And we have an excellent fence."

"Good point, Eva—but he'll live inside with us, of course. Big dogs especially need companionship."

Cade shook his head, but he was smiling. "You're actually serious?"

"Like a heart attack!" Emily yelled. Noelle shot her a startled look.

"She's been talking to my dad a lot," Cade said in way of explanation. "I don't think he knows what to do with himself these days."

"Auntie Jo's waiting for a call back," Eva prodded.

Emily wide-eyed them, hopefully. "Soooo?"

Cade twined his fingers through Noelle's. "I know we've been trying to make most decisions together lately," Cade said. "But this one's all yours. Whatever you want."

"Well . . . the only reason I really, really never wanted a dog was that we were all running around so much—and that's not really an issue anymore—plus they make it impossible to keep an immaculate house."

Emily's face fell. Eva looked glum.

"And since I'd much rather we all live happily in our house than have it be some show place, I think . . . we're getting a dog."

Noelle made a show of plugging her ears as the kids cheered, then picked up the phone and called Jo.

The details came together with surprising ease. Baby brother Brian was apparently having some "lady issues" (Surprise, surprise, Noelle thought) and was taking a leave from work and heading out of town indefinitely. Noelle felt bad about the sarcastic thought the minute she had it. If Brian was leaving work, it was serious—and maybe had more to do with the awkward situation Caren and Duncan put him in than his personal life. She could only imagine how they'd both try to tear him back and forth. He'd happily deliver their new family member on Dave's behalf.

Jo laughed hard when she heard Hammer would henceforth be called Henry.

"There's one thing I don't understand," Noelle said just before the call wrapped up.

"What's that?" Jo asked.

"I thought you guys and Dave were mortal enemies. What's with him coming to you to help find a home for Henry?"

There was a second's hesitation, then Jo spoke, sounding troubled or even deeply sad. "Well, let's just say I feel badly for Dave. He's not one hundred percent terrible—oh, shoot, there's a delivery guy. I've got to run. I'll fill you in later."

"Sounds good, and please thank him very much for us. We'll take good care of Henry, er . . . Hammer. We'll love him a lot."

As Noelle hung up, Cade wrapped his arms around her and kissed her temple. "You know how folks say 'never change' to people they love?" he asked.

"Uh huh?"

"I get what they mean because when you love someone you want your love to remain static, to stay the same . . . but you were right. Love can't last without change. Everything changes whether we want it to or not." He kissed her jaw. Then her mouth.

"Ugh, you guys are gross," Eva complained, but there was happy note in her voice. "I'm going online to look at leashes and dog beds." She and Emily left the room.

"I like how we've changed so far, and I look forward to whatever's next," Cade added.

"*But*?" Noelle asked, unsure about what to expect, yet feeling strangely at ease.

"But some things will never change."

"Oh, yeah? Like what?"

"Like I love you—and I always will." Cade pulled her close and she leaned into the solid wall of him.

"Well, okay," she said. "I think I can live with that."

Dear Reader,

I know a romance novel featuring a long married couple is a little unusual, but the more Noelle and Cade whispered in my ear, the more I felt their pain, admired their hope and burned to tell their story. Besides, falling in love, wonderful as it is, is only ever half the story. Managing to stay in love is the never-ending series!

Anyway, I hoped you enjoyed *Spoons* as much as I did—and that you, like me, want to spend more time at River's Sigh B & B. If the series is new to you, I hope you'll check out the other books: *Wedding Bands*, *Hooked*, and *One To Keep*. And if you're itching to know what's up with Brian or how life will go for Aisha, keep an eye out. They'll each have their own book later in 2016!

I'd love to hear from you, so please visit **www.evbishop.com**, sign up for my newsletter, find me on Facebook or follow my Tweets (Ev_Bishop). And on a similar note, reviews really, really help authors. Please consider leaving a rating and a few kind words on Amazon, GoodReads, your blog, Facebook, or anywhere else you like to hang out when your nose isn't in a book. Thank you so much for reading.

Wishing you love and laughter and great reads,

Ev Bishop

Curious about Jo and Callum and the birth of River's Sigh B & B? For a peek at WEDDING BANDS, the story that started it all, read on. . . .

The Past

JO SAT ON THE CHILLY metal bench under the grimy shelter in front of the bus station for as long as she could, kicking up gravel with the scuffed toes of her sneakers and drawing designs on the fogged up glass. Where was he, where was he, where was he?

She doodled her and Callum's names inside a heart-shaped flourish, then scrawled "True if erased!" beside it.

When she couldn't hold still any longer, Jo hopped to her feet and paced, not wanting to go inside the building because what if he arrived and thought she was the one who hadn't shown up? But it was raining harder now, and cold wind blew sheets of water into the shelter. She could care less if she was soaked to the skin usually, but the long bus ride would be uncomfortable if her jeans were soggy. Plus, she had to pee. Really bad.

She considered the cozy interior of the station—well, cozy by comparison to where she was now anyway—once more. Then looked up the street and down it. Callum's red Honda Civic was still nowhere to be seen. And anyway, he'd said he was going to walk. It was getting darker, but there were streetlights. She could see all too well there was no one walking toward her in any direction. She cracked her knuckles. The movement sparkled under the streetlight, and she looked down at the delicate gold band on her left ring finger. A tiny diamond twinkled up at her. She rubbed it with her thumb and grinned.

"Callum," she whispered. Then she laughed out loud. "Callum, hurry up!"

It boggled her mind that they were doing this. They were really doing this. They were running away to get married!

But at 9:30, Callum still hadn't shown up and the bus was supposed to board at 9:48. Jo's bottom lip had a raw groove in it from her teeth. A slow but steady trickle of people filed past her into the station to buy tickets, ship boxes, and say good-bye to departing family and friends. Jo's bladder moved past discomfort. It was going to burst. And her heart might too.

She headed into the station and beelined to the washroom. The stall was cramped but clean. She relieved herself without finding any real relief at all. Why hadn't he come? Where was he?

She made her way to the payphones on the back wall by the vending machines. Her sister Sam said one day people would have miniature phones they'd carry on them at all times to call people whenever they wanted. Jo always thought that was far-fetched. Who on earth had so many people to call that they couldn't wait till they got home? But tonight, picking up the gummy receiver, she changed her mind. Personal phones weren't a terrible idea. Maybe Sam was onto something.

Jo inserted her quarter and pressed each digit in Callum's phone number with utmost care, like she was performing a ritual or charm that would bring them together—or not.

The phone rang once, rang twice—was answered midway through the third ring by a clipped, impatient voice. "Yes?"

Rats. Mr. Archer. Callum's dad. He hated her.

"Um, hello, Mr. Archer?"

No acknowledgement that yes, it was him. Not even a grunt.

"Is Callum there, please?"

Mr. Archer's voice warmed suddenly. "Is this you Tracey?"

"Um, no—"

"Oh, I'm sorry. Selene?"

"No, I'm—"

A chuckle interrupted her. "Sorry, sorry. You know how it is for an old dad, trying to keep up with a young buck's does."

A young buck's does? Jo traced a crack in the tile with her toe. What a creep.

"It's Jo," she said, "Jo Kendall."

"Oh, sorry, lad—thought you were a girl for a minute. Must be a poor connection."

Jo exhaled. Her knuckles were white on the receiver. "We've met, Mr. Archer. I've been dating Callum all year."

"Oh, *oh* . . . " There was a shuffling sound, then a porcelain clank, like a plate dropped too quickly onto another. "Well, I don't keep track. He took off with someone in a blue Volkswagen about an hour ago. I just assumed the driver was the girl in his life these days. That's not you? Not your car?"

Jo bowed her head and mumbled into the mouthpiece, "No, not me. Thanks anyway. We'll probably all meet up at the same place later." She hoped she didn't sound as miserable as she felt. Who wanted to give the horrible man the satisfaction that she'd been ditched?

She hung the phone back in place, but stayed by the booth a moment, heels of her hands pressed into her eyes. What should she do? There was another bus at 5:30 a.m. Should she try to round Callum up? But on foot in the pouring rain in the growing darkness? She had no idea where to even start to look. Greenridge had a small population, sure, but it was scattered over a huge geographic area. At the very least, she should call Ray. Of course she should! Obviously Callum would've called to say he was held up. He wasn't an asshole.

Breathing easier, she dug for another quarter.

"Yeah-lo," a raspy voice answered.

Jo smiled at the familiar, corny combination of "Yeah and hello" her uncle always used.

"Hey, Uncle Ray. It's Jo. Has Callum called by any chance?"

"He sure did, kiddo. Sounded kinda upset. I took a message. Let me see. . . . "

Jo waited for Ray to rummage through his head for scraps of the conversation, a familiar, confusing mixture of love and irritation swirling in her gut. She prayed he hadn't hit the bottle too heavy already, or who knew what mixed up, incoherent babble he'd pass on.

But Ray didn't sound overly tipsy and wasn't slurring when he said, "Ah, here it is, princess."

Jo rolled her eyes. Her uncle was the only person in the world who looked at her and saw a princess.

"I wrote it down."

"Wow, will wonders never cease?" The words slipped out before she could stop them.

Uncle Ray only laughed. "Wait a minute, I thought you said you were Jo? How come you're sounding like your big sister Sam?"

Jo shifted from one foot to the other. It was 9:39. People streamed out of the small station toward the big Greyhound rumbling outside.

"He said, um . . . " Jo could practically see Ray squinting at his barely legible scrawl. "He's sorry, but it's over. It won't work—repeated that three times, angry-like. 'It won't work—just won't work.' Does

273

that make any sense?"

Jo closed her eyes and squeezed the bridge of her nose. It made no sense. It also made perfect sense. She could hardly speak. "Yeah, yeah, it does. Thanks."

"Call me when you get settled back at your mom's, all right?"

Jo forced a few more words out. "Yes, yes, I will."

"I love you, baby girl."

The words coaxed a blurry-eyed smile. Oh, Uncle Ray. "I love you too." And she did, but like everything in her life, it was so damned complicated. How could you love someone and not really ever be there for them? Never get your shit together? You'd think with her history, Jo would be used to it by now, but she wasn't. Some day she was going to have a home. A real one. A non-temporary, longer than a summer or a school year place to stay. She and Callum both wanted that—or then again, maybe not. Maybe just she did. She alone. Again.

She swallowed hard and stared up at the ceiling, willing the tide of saltwater in her eyes to recede. She pressed a hand to her sickish-feeling stomach. What was she going to do?

A crackly voice came over the P.A. system and announced last call for eastbound travellers.

Her suitcase was already stowed in the belly of the bus, loaded while she'd sat around waiting. It would be hard to change her mind now, even if she wanted to—and did she want to? Did she want to wander around the small town all summer, facing memories of Callum everywhere? Did she want to have some big high-drama face off with him about the how and why of him calling everything off so randomly and so last minute? No, she just couldn't. It was too hard. And Ray's, much as she loved him, wasn't the place for her anymore. Things were going from bad to worse for him—and she'd just turned eighteen, just graduated. She was too young to settle down to take care of her uncle who was drinking himself to death and refused help. Even through the pain, she knew that.

She took a deep breath, hoisted her backpack, then limped outside as if physically injured. It felt like she was. On her way toward the silver-haired bus driver who stood by the bus door collecting tickets, she passed by the shelter. The blurred words "Callum + Jo, forever. True if erased!" jumped off the glass at her. Out of habit, she lifted her hand to rub the words away, then realized how dumb she was. Her hand returned to her queasy stomach. She boarded the bus.

Chapter 1

The Present

THE EVENING AIR WAS CRISP but not yet freezing. Jo stopped in her tracks just to inhale. The comforting scent of cedar smoke from the house's chimney, the salty-sweet smell of smoking salmon, and the earthy fragrance of the changing season thrilled through her. She wanted to pinch herself. It was all really hers— well, *theirs*. Her sister Samantha would see the light eventually. Imagine living here all year round. It would be like a postcard every season. All the work was worth it. How could Samantha want to get rid of this place? Was she crazy?

The first fallen leaves gleamed gold against the dark lawn and crackled under her boots as she continued toward the old house. The porch light glowed a friendly welcome, though its beam created shadows around her that she wouldn't have noticed if there'd been no light at all.

Jo climbed the three steps to the home's wraparound porch, and leaned her trout rod against a wall, well out of the way of the door. She was careful to make sure the pretty—and more importantly, lucky—wedding band lure, a bright beaded thing encrusted with rhinestones, was safely held in one of the rod's eyes. She tucked her tackle box beside the rod and carried her basket of treasure into the house. Fresh caught Rainbows—even their name was gorgeous. She whispered a prayer of thanks for the beauty and bounty of the area. Her stomach rumbled.

Jo whistled for Hoover, but the dog didn't come. He was probably still by the river, roaming about. She crossed her fingers that he hadn't found something disgusting to roll in—his favorite trick—and whistled again. Still nothing. Used to his selective hearing and even more selective obedience, she happily transitioned to thoughts of side dishes. Asparagus and oven-roasted baby potatoes? Rice pilaf and broccoli rabe? Mmmm.

She kicked off her rubber boots and left them where they fell. Yes, they blocked the door, but wasn't that one of the luxuries of living alone? The time would come soon enough when she had to worry about appearances and keeping everything just so. She imagined a houseful of paying guests and smiled.

She left her old black and red checked flannel jacket on. She'd get the fish frying before she cleaned up.

Halfway down the darkened hall toward the kitchen, Jo's stomach tightened. There was a light on—and she knew she'd turned them all off.

"Hello?" she called, and felt stupid when she realized she'd clutched the buck knife attached to her belt. What was she going to do? Stab an intruder?

"Hello," she said again, louder.

The voice that answered almost stopped her heart.

"Jo—is that you, finally? I've been waiting all night. Where were you?"

Jo relaxed her grip on the knife handle reluctantly. If there was someone she actually wouldn't mind stabbing it would be—

"Come on, don't you have a kiss for your sis?"

—Yep, her "sis." Samantha.

Jo flipped a switch, and another feeble bulb lit up. It didn't do much to brighten the wood panel hall, but would keep Jo from colliding with Sam—or colliding literally, anyway. That was the first of many things Samantha complained about regarding the cabin they'd inherited from their uncle: its "archaic" lighting.

Samantha's high heels clacked across the hardwood floor in the living room, then moved into the kitchen. Jo cringed, envisioning the dints she was probably leaving in her wake.

"Good grief, Jo. It's a tomb in here. How do you stand it?"

Had she called it or what? "Every bulb doesn't have to glare. I like soft—"

"What's in the basket?"

How Jo wished she could disappear into one of the bedrooms, any one of them, no matter how cluttered or unfinished. But as she knew from a lifetime of experience, it wouldn't help. Samantha would be there, in her face, until she tired of chewing at whatever she was after this time—and since "this time" involved money, she wouldn't drop the bone till the cash was in hand.

"Trout," Jo admitted miserably, all fantasies of a candlelit dinner for one dashed to hell.

"Gross."

Jo shrugged. If only that opinion meant Samantha was planning to eat elsewhere—but Jo knew better than that. She headed for the counter beneath the big window that had a gorgeous mountain view, and dumped her catch into one of the stainless steel sinks. "Dot's doing Italian specials all week."

"Pasta? Like I'd eat pasta. Goes straight to your belly."

Jo patted her own "belly" with affection, not caring if she got fish slime on her shirt. It was due for a wash. "Well, I'm making potatoes."

Samantha followed her, keeping a safe three-foot distance from any potential food mess. She gave Jo a quick once over and frowned.

"What are you wearing? You stink like fresh air and you look like a lumberjack. And tonight of all nights!"

"What do you mean 'tonight'? What's so special about *tonight*?"

Jo scrubbed her hands and started peeling potatoes. Samantha sighed dramatically. "I was hoping you'd look human when you met my lawyer, but thankfully I've already warned him about you."

"Your *what*? Here, now—*what?*"

Samantha flourished one hand. "Callum, we're ready for you." A shadow moved in the dining room.

Crap.

Jo was so angry she could hardly see.

And then she was so startled she almost sliced her thumb with the potato peeler. She put it down. *Callum*? As in Callum Archer? Her old Callum? No . . . the first name was a coincidence. Had to be. A tall man walked out of the living room and extended his hand.

"Callum Archer," Samantha said and Jo's brain swam. "Josephine—or Jo, as she's sometimes called—my sister."

Jo tried to give the hand gripping hers a firm shake, but as she met his piercing aqua blue eyes—eyes she'd never forget—she started to freak out. An irrational observation hit her: the man, Sam's lawyer, *her old Callum*, had strong sexy-rough hands for a guy work-ing a desk job. Her stomach churned. Breathe, she commanded herself. *Breathe*. It was absolutely no comfort at all that he looked as shocked as she felt.

"Hello Callum," she said, hoping desperately for a dry, casual tone. "It's been a long time." And it had been. Fifteen years, four months. Not that she'd counted. . . .

"*Jo*? I'll be damned." And Callum did look like he'd just been damned. All the blood drained from his already fair skin, making his blue eyes burn even brighter and his black hair seem all the blacker. "You look exactly the same," he said.

"When it's half dark, perhaps," Jo said wryly. "But thanks." So he was still a flatterer. That much hadn't changed.

Samantha's eagle sharp gaze darted to Callum, then speared Jo. "So what—you guys know each other?"

Jo raised her eyebrows and shook her head. "Uh, no. I wouldn't say that really. Used to. A bit. Kind of."

"Kind of," Callum repeated with a bitter note in his voice that Jo didn't understand—and that pissed her off. What the hell did he have to be bitter about?

There was a moment of uneasy silence, then Callum had the nerve to laugh. "Sisters. Wow." Jo hated the sexy, low timber of his voice and his easy confidence. "Here I'd just assumed the Josephine Kendall everyone in town was talking about, and that you went on about, was some aunt or something. I didn't link *Jo* to Josephine at all."

"Well, it's a terrible name, but it's better than *Jo*," Samantha said.

"She doesn't really strike me as the next thing to a bag lady," Callum said, his head tilting as he studied Jo.

The next thing to a bag lady? What on earth had Sam been telling people?

Samantha sounded as affronted as Jo felt. "Have

you taken a good look at her?"

Callum was still gripping Jo's hand and she yanked away, suddenly conscious of her muddy jeans, old man's shirt, and—no doubt—leaf and branch strewn hair. Shit. She was making an excellent first impression as a business professional, able to single-handedly turn the old cabin and overgrown property into a successful bed-and-breakfast, wasn't she? She could practically hear Samantha's victory chant.

She tried to fight the heat rising to her cheeks but failed, imagining how the room looked from his eyes. Breakfast and lunch dishes piled messily by the sink. A mishmash of junk littering the floor by the dishwasher. . . . She'd meant to box it up for Goodwill, but the beautiful fall afternoon had called to her. And what kind of ignoramus shows up unannounced and basically breaks into someone's house anyway?

"I'm not sure what my sister told you, or why either of you thought an impromptu, unscheduled appointment would be at all appropriate or beneficial"—she glared at Samantha for a moment—"but it's neither of those things. It's a Friday night, and I have plans. We can set up a time next week to meet at your office to discuss the estate and terms of my uncle's will, or, if you're from out of town, we can conference call."

Oh-so-confident Callum looked startled, and Jo made a couple more observations, all equally irritating. Time had been more than kind to him. While she'd found him gorgeous, like a rock god or something, back in the day—his tall, lanky frame had filled out with age. He looked more like a professional athlete than what her mind conjured for a lawyer. His icy blue eyes were still penetrating—and stood out spectacularly against his shock of silky raven hair—but he had just the start of crinkling laugh lines that softened his intensity. And he smelled good. Like fresh baked cookies, vanilla, cinnamon—

Callum's voice, sharp and irritated, cut through the buttery attraction melting through Jo. "You didn't arrange this? We just surprised her?" he said to Samantha.

Samantha waved her hand dismissively, and Jo wished she could lop one of those constantly gesturing hands right off. "She would've stalled indefinitely. And she doesn't really have plans. She's having dinner *by herself.*"

Like it's a capital crime or something, Jo thought.

Callum cleared his throat. "Sounds nice, actually. I'm sorry for the misunderstanding—sorry we disturbed you."

Jo didn't lie and say it was fine. She herded them to the door.

"I don't know why you're being like this. We need to talk, get this figured out, decide what works best for everyone."

"We have talked, Samantha. We disagree on what 'works best' means. Your lawyer may call me next week, anytime Monday through Friday between nine and five. I'll consult my schedule and we can set an appointment."

"Your *schedule?*" Samantha mocked.

Callum placed a hand low on Samantha's back and guided her toward the door. "She's right, Samantha. This wasn't the right way to proceed."

"And just so you're aware. If you break into my house again, I'll call the cops and press charges."

Callum turned back from the door. "I'm not sure it's so simple as 'your' house, Jo—but again, my apologies for the intrusion. It was a misunderstanding. I'll be in touch."

"Jo—"

"Let's just go, Samantha."

"Yes, *go*, Samantha. Take your slimy lawyer's advice. That's what you're paying him for right?"

Jo leaned against the mudroom's wall after they left and closed her eyes. Why had she been so rude? Yes, even after all these years, the very thought of Callum was a slicing barb—but that was no excuse. They'd been kids. She needed to let him off the hook. For her own sake, not just his.

What's next for Callum and Jo?
Read WEDDING BANDS,
Book 1 in the River's Sigh B & B series today.

About the Author

 **Ev Bishop** is a longtime columnist with the *Terrace Standard,* and her other non-fiction articles and essays have been published across North America. Her true love, however, is fiction, and she writes in a variety of lengths and genres. If you're a short story lover or read other genres alongside romance, visit **www.evbishop.com** to learn more.

Some short story publications include: "Not All Magic is Nice," *Pulp Literature*, "The Picture Book," *Every Day Fiction Magazine*, "Riddles," *100 Stories for Queensland,* "On the Wall," *Every Day Fiction Magazine,* "My Mom is a Freak," *Cleavage: Breakaway Fiction for Real Girls*, "HVS," "Red Bird," and "Wishful," (available through Ether Books).

Novels include *Bigger Things*, *Wedding Bands*, Book 1 in the River's Sigh B & B series, *Hooked*, Book 2 in the River's Sigh B & B series, *Spoons*, Book 3 in the River's Sigh B & B series, and *New Year's Resolution: One to Keep*, a River's Sigh B & B novella. She also writes romance under the pen name Toni Sheridan (*The Present* and *Drummer Boy*).

www.ingramcontent.com/pod-product-compliance
Lightning Source LLC
Chambersburg PA
CBHW070739180626
46818CB00007B/2918